CW01676536

Rosie & The Troll

by

Ross F Lindsay

Copyright © Ross Lindsay 2021

All rights reserved in all media. No part of this publication may be reproduced, stored in retrieval system, copied in any form or by any means, electronic, mechanical, photocopying, recording or otherwise transmitted without written permission from the author and/or publisher. You must not circulate this book in any format. Any person who does any unauthorised act in relation to this publication may be liable to criminal prosecution and civil claims for damages.

This novel is a work of fiction. Names, characters, businesses, places, events and incidents are either the products of the author's imagination or used in a fictitious manner. Any resemblance to actual persons, living or dead, or actual events is purely coincidental.

Produced in United Kingdom.

Author and Cover Design: Ross F Lindsay
Editorial Services: www.bookeditingservices.co.uk

ISBN: 9789403624334
For permission requests, please contact:
ross.lindsay@logiprom.co.uk

Sponsored by

For Rosie, our first grandchild.

Chapter 1 The Old Rustic Bridge

Rosie was staying with Grandma for the weekend. The summer holidays were coming to an end, and she would soon be back at school. Her younger sister, Mollie, would usually accompany her; however, this weekend Mollie was staying with a friend for a birthday sleepover.

It was a bright and breezy Saturday afternoon, and Rosie was walking to Grandma's from her house. It wasn't far. She had her walking boots on, a pair of jeans, a T-shirt and a coat. Being late August, it wasn't cold, just a little chilly in the wind. She was looking forward to chatting with Grandma. She often told wonderful stories about her father, Rosie's great-grandad, about some amazing adventures he'd had with an imaginary Troll when he was a boy.

She'd never met her great-grandad, he died quite young, long before Rosie was born, but she almost felt as though she knew him – the stories Grandma told were so vivid and magical. They really stirred her imagination. She fantasised about being involved in some of his adventures on an alien planet out there amongst the stars.

"Hello, Grandma," she shouted as she opened the cottage door and went inside. Hattie, Grandma's black Labrador, came charging down the hall barking excitedly. "Hello, Hattie, how are you today? Shall we go for a walk later?" Hattie raised her head and barked again; she understood the word "walk" very well.

Rosie loved her walks in the woods behind Grandma's house. Various paths stretched for miles into the North Yorkshire moorland, a vast expanse of rolling hills and trails, lined by flowering bushes and shrubs and cocooned by enormous trees.

"Hello, Rosie," said Grandma as she came out of the kitchen. "That's good timing. I've just been baking some scones and they've just come out of the oven. Did Mollie go to her party?"

"Yes, she did, she's very excited. They're going horse riding this afternoon."

"Ooh lovely," said Grandma. "Go and sit outside, darling, I'll bring out some tea."

Grandma lived in a lovely little cottage at the end of a farm track. It backed onto the moorland with a large, wooded area immediately behind it.

Rosie walked through the house filled with the tantalising smell of baking and stepped out into the garden. She sat down on a garden chair and leant on the little table. Staring down the path at the small wild garden, she listened to the birds and stroked Hattie's head. The dog had taken a position by Rosie's feet; she was also waiting for the scones.

As Grandma came out with a tray filled with the scrumptious fresh baking and a pot of tea, Hattie sat up immediately.

"You can wait your turn, Hattie," said Grandma. "Our guest goes first."

The young girl laughed at the dog who was staring directly at the tray of scones in anticipation. She broke off a little piece and gave it to her. "I'll take her out for a walk in the woods, Grandma."

"Oh, she'll love that, thank you, Rosie. I think your dad may pop around later, so I don't want to miss him."

"It's no problem. I love to walk in the woods – it's so peaceful," she replied. "Grandma?" asked Rosie. "Where do you think your dad got all his ideas from about the Troll stories?"

"I don't know. He just came out with them, one after another. I told him that he should write them all down, but he never would. I've told you as many as I can remember."

"They just seem so real," said Rosie.

"Yes," said Grandma. "He was always a good storyteller. You remind me of him, Rosie, your mannerisms and imagination."

Rosie ate as many scones as she could manage. "I feel really stuffed now, Grandma; they were lovely. I'd better go for that walk – I'm sure it will do us both good." Hattie was still looking greedily at the plate. "No more for you, Hattie. You'll get fat."

"Okay, darling," said Grandma. "I'll clear up. You get going whilst the sun's still out."

Rosie came out of the back gate with Hattie and headed along the familiar lane between the trees. The dog ambled along behind her sniffing the vegetation and biting off blades of grass. Every now and then she coughed and snorted.

"You'll choke one of these days." The dog looked up at Rosie with her big brown eyes, said nothing and walked on.

It was a pleasant day, although she could tell the summer was coming to an end. A change in the air and a few leaves were already falling from the trees. The breeze made shadows flow backwards and forwards across the path, and small birds competed noisily with their repetitive songs. They strolled along the path in silence, both daydreaming. Hattie probably about more scones, and Rosie was thinking about friends and the new school term a few days away.

About twenty minutes into the walk, Rosie noticed Hattie acting a little strangely. The dog was standing frozen on the spot and peering along the track towards the old stone bridge.

"What's up, Hattie?"

The dog turned her head to look at Rosie. It was an odd little bridge, lonely and overgrown. It was made of large rough-cut stones, and underneath was a long, dark tunnel. Grandad had told Rosie it was something to do with the old ironstone workings; the track they were on was once used as a light railway.

"Come on, Hattie. What's the matter?" Rosie couldn't see what she was looking at so decided to ignore her. She continued along the path towards the bridge. After a time, she realised that Hattie was still not with her. She stopped and looked back as the dog often disappeared into the bushes to search for something of interest. She saw her about fifty metres away, still standing in the same place looking at her or perhaps staring right past her. When their eyes made contact, Hattie started barking.

"Hattie, you're scaring me!" Rosie looked around nervously. She was standing in the middle of the little bridge. Trees towered all around her. It was darker here, damp and a bit fusty.

"Hello, Rosie," said a deep, gruff voice. Rosie got quite a fright.

"Who's that?" she shrieked. The voice was coming from underneath the bridge, perhaps from the tunnel.

"Don't be frightened," said the voice. "I'm a friend."

Rosie stood still, but her legs wanted to run back down the path towards Hattie. She stopped herself. If the voice stayed under the bridge, she knew she could easily run away.

"I don't have any friends who hide under bridges in the woods and sound like you."

"Well," said the voice, "that's a good point. We haven't met before. I've been waiting for you." Rosie was alarmed and confused all at the same time.

"Look," said Rosie, "my dog doesn't seem to like you. I think I need to go."

"No, no, please don't," said the voice, which was now sounding a little anxious. "You're right, a dog can sense me; it confuses them you see. I promise I won't harm her."

"What do you want from me? And why can't I see you?"

"Well," said the voice, "I've been waiting here for you. I have an important task for you. I need you to close the gate."

"Gate, what gate?" asked Rosie. The strange gruff voice spoke again.

"It's a gate I opened with your great-grandfather Michael over seventy years ago. It's still open you see, and I need you to help me close it."

"Look," she said, "I don't know what you're talking about. I'm confused, and why won't Hattie come to me?"

At that moment, Hattie trotted the fifty metres towards Rosie, sat down and stared up at her.

Rosie opened her mouth to speak but couldn't think of anything to say, so she tried again. "Are you talking about my great-grandad Michael?"

"Yes, oh yes," said the gruff voice, which now sounded excited. "A lovely lad and a good friend of mine. He was special, like you."

"Sorry, what do you mean by special?"

"Well, Michael and you are in a long line of human children from your family, going back generations. It's only the special ones who can open or close the gate."

"Stop," she said. "Can we start from the beginning? What's your name?"

"Ah yes, quite right," said the voice. "I'm known as Thumblerock on my world. Your great-grandfather used to call me Rocky. I come from a race of Trolls. Not the scary monsters you might imagine in your books. No, no, we are nothing like that at all."

"A Troll, my world?" Rosie was becoming increasingly anxious.

"Now, now, Rosie, don't get all aeriated. I don't want to frighten you. If we could meet, face to face so's to speak, I'll explain?"

"Oh, I'm not sure about that," she said.

"Don't worry," said the Troll. "You stay up there, and I'll stay down here."

Before Rosie could answer, there was a crunching of leaves and twigs as something began to move out from the tunnel under the bridge.

"Don't scream when you see me," said the Troll. "I may look a little strange to you."

Rosie and Hattie peered nervously over the rickety fence into the little gorge below that led into the tunnel.

A large, hairy creature wearing a brown duffel coat with bright gold toggles, a hood and large black square-ended boots walked slowly out into the light, turned around and looked up towards them.

His bootstraps were wrapped around his hairy legs up to green knee-length moleskin trousers. He had a wide and bumpy face with a large nose and bright fluorescent green eyes. His hair was jet black and straggly and flowed down onto his shoulders.

Rosie was shocked by his appearance. She remained as calm as she could. It was like looking at a cartoon character. Hattie grumbled and barked. She was about to ask Rosie something, but thought better of it, and then trotted down towards the Troll.

"Hattie, Hattie!" Rosie shouted, but it was too late. Hattie was already with the Troll, sniffing at his boots.

"Hello, old girl," said the Troll. He knelt to give Hattie something to chew from his coat pocket. Hattie looked up at the Troll, grumbled and looked back at Rosie. "Hattie says she likes you a lot, but you don't bring enough treats when you go out for a walk." Rosie's mouth fell wide open.

"Are you serious, you can understand what she's saying?"

"Oh yes," said the Troll. "On our world all the animals can talk with each other. Some not much, and some never stop talking – drives you bononkers."

"Bononkers," said Rosie. "Don't you mean bonkers?"

"No, no, I don't think so. If it's all right now, can you come down and talk to me under the bridge? I could be seen out there."

"Oh," she said. "That sounds a bit scary. I'm not quite sure I want to do that. I need to be back at Grandma's for tea you see." Rosie looked at her watch. "In fact, we're already late – she'll be worried."

"Oh, yes, of course, we don't want your grandma worrying," said the Troll, scratching his head. "I'm sorry, Rosie, I don't do this often. The last time I was here on Earth was when I met your great-grandad." Rosie suddenly gasped.

"You're the Troll in my great-grandad's stories. I thought they were just make-believe. They can't be true?"

"Well, I'm here and yes, I expect all his stories were true. I loved your great-grandad from the first time I met him. I hope we can become good friends, too. It's now your turn, Rosie, to come with me I mean."

"To go with you where? To your planet?" asked Rosie in a muted, nervous voice.

"I know it's a bit of a shock for you and a lot to take in," said the Troll. "Let me think now. If you prefer, how about we meet again at the same time tomorrow? To give you some time to think about it."

Rosie looked at her watch again – it was half past four.

"There's one small thing you can do for me, Rosie," said the Troll. "Can you ask your grandma about a little silver box your great-grandad had? Don't tell her you've met me, though. No, that wouldn't do at all."

"I could I suppose," she said.

"Yes, good, good," said the Troll. "I'll be here waiting for you." He turned and walked back into the tunnel muttering to himself. She could hear his heavy footsteps crunching, and then she thought she heard a faint tinkling of little bells, then silence.

Hattie rejoined Rosie on top of the bridge, and they started to walk back down the forest path towards Grandma's.

"What was all that about, Hattie?" She felt a little shaken by the encounter. It all happened so fast; she couldn't make much sense of it. Hattie looked up at her, barked then whimpered, then stopped and looked back towards the bridge. "I know. I'm sorry. You liked him, and he said he could talk to you. That's very weird or amazing, especially for you. I just need to be careful. I can't quite believe what we've just seen. He said he was a Troll, and he wants me to close a gate. That's a peculiar request from a strange-looking creature. Perhaps I should ask Grandma? No, I can't. He told me not to and it may scare her. Maybe her dad, Michael, mentioned something about the little silver box. Who knows, it's all just bononkers, as the Troll said!"

Rosie opened the gate into Grandma's garden and followed the path by the willow trees and past the pond.

They came around the corner and saw Grandma looking up the garden towards them.

"Ahh, at last," she said. "I was starting to worry." Hattie dashed into the kitchen. "Don't worry, Hattie, your tea is out," she said as the dog pushed past her legs to get to her food bowl.

Rosie sat down at the garden table, which was once again full with sandwiches and cakes.

"Have a sandwich," said Grandma. "Was it a nice walk? You look a little pale. Are you feeling all right? Has something happened?"

"I'm fine, don't worry." Grandma put her cup down and frowned.

"What is it, then? Tell me, sweetheart?"

"Grandma," said Rosie, "your dad, Michael, all those stories he told you about the Trolls when he was a young boy. Do you think he may have really met one?"

"Of course not. It's all just stories. There's no such thing as Trolls. He made it all up to entertain us when we were kids." She started laughing and clapping her hands. "Such magical tales." Grandma looked back at Rosie; she could see small tears rolling down her cheeks. "What is it? Has something upset you?"

Rosie wiped her eyes on her sleeve and smiled. Knowing she mustn't worry Grandma, as she would get upset if Rosie told her that she'd met a strange, hairy Troll in the woods, she decided to concoct a little white lie and try to find out as much as she could from Grandma about the Troll stories.

"Did you or Uncle Tim once tell us a story about the Troll and a little silver box? Another story that your dad told you all when you were children? It was a lovely story. I would've loved to have met my great-grandad."

"I wish you could have, too, Rosie; he would have loved you all so much. That's just reminded me," said Grandma. "Now that is a funny thing, in your great-grandad's will, he left a little silver box with an instruction to pass it on to one of my grandchildren. I thought it odd at the time. The instruction was to give it to the first one of you who asked about the Trolls and the little silver box. I'd quite forgotten about it; you've jogged my memory. Let me see if I can find it. I know I have it stored safely somewhere. Perhaps it will cheer you up."

Grandma jumped up from the table and went into the house. Rosie watched as she disappeared inside. It was best if she didn't tell Grandma about her meeting with a Troll in the woods. The shock of finding out that her dad's stories may have been true all along could be a bit much for her. *No*, she thought, *best to keep the secret*. Great-grandad kept it secret, disguising it as stories, so for the moment that was good enough for Rosie.

Hattie came outside and lay down by her feet. She looked up at Rosie and started to grumble.

"You're talking to me again, aren't you? I bet you're asking me if we're going back to see the Troll tomorrow. I don't mind telling you that I'm scared and excited all at the same time. This has been a strange experience for both of us. I feel connected in some way, almost as if I've been waiting for something to happen. I think we probably should go back in memory of great-grandad, to find out what this is all about."

Grandma reappeared at the back door with an excited smile on her face.

"Here it is, Rosie, here it is. As you're the first of my grandchildren to have mentioned the silver box, then you must have it. I've kept it all these years at the back of my wardrobe. I'd quite forgotten about it. I can't imagine why he was being so mysterious. There you go, that was your great-grandad for you."

She passed a small dark green velvet bag to Rosie. It was secured by a gold braided drawstring, which was tied in a little bow. The idea that this small bag held part of a puzzle she was now involved in was quite unbelievable. Her hands trembled as she carefully tugged at the string and pulled the bow apart. Was she imagining it? Could she feel a tingling in her fingers and hear a faint ringing of tiny bells? Just like the bells she thought she'd heard earlier when the Troll went back into the tunnel?

Her heart was pounding as she carefully tipped up the bag. A small, ornate but tarnished silver box slid out onto the palm of her hand. Instantly, the box started shimmering silver, then blue, then purple, then yellow – one beautiful colour after the other. Rosie jumped inwardly; all the colours of the rainbow were washing over it in waves. Her whole hand tingled with static electricity, like tiny little pinpricks.

Rosie suddenly realised that Grandma was peering over her shoulder; she'd quite forgotten that she was there.

"Just an old silver box," said Grandma. "I can't imagine what all the fuss was about?" She picked it out of her granddaughter's hand and turned it over a few times. Instantly, the colours and the ringing faded. Rosie realised that Grandma was not seeing or hearing anything from the box at all. "Anyway, it's yours now," and she passed it back.

"Thank you, Grandma. I love it – it's wonderful."

"He wanted you to have it, so there it is." Grandma sat down in her chair, rubbed Hattie's head and drifted away into her own thoughts as she stared down the garden.

Rosie examined the little box in the palm of her hand. Once again, it started to radiate its colourful light and tinkle a soft sound of tiny distant bells. Each time she put it down, it returned to a dormant state. She picked it up again. *There must be something inside*, she thought and turned the box over and over, looking for some way of opening it. It was tightly sealed, so eventually she gave up.

"Well, Rosie, the sun is going down and it's turned a little chilly. Let's go inside," said Grandma.

Hattie got up slowly and stretched from head to toe before letting out a grunt and heading for the back door.

"I'm sure that dog understands every word we say," said Grandma.

Rosie, Hattie and Grandma spent the evening in front of the fire where they chatted about their family. Rosie quizzed her with as many questions as she could think of, trying to uncover some more information about her great-grandad. Grandma told her as much as she could remember, but it didn't really provide any answers to the questions churning through Rosie's head.

She lay in bed that night staring at the ceiling in the room Grandma had prepared for her weekend stay. Hattie was with her; she loved the attention when Rosie came to stay. Rosie's concentration was broken when Hattie started snoring loudly, which made her giggle. It was comforting in a way. If Hattie wasn't troubled by the Troll, perhaps she shouldn't be.

Chapter 2 Blinded by the Light

Thumblerock had returned to the bleak moon, the halfway place between his world and Earth. All these worlds were linked by an invisible web. The connection was fragile. Any imbalance could have a detrimental effect across the whole network, and a threat was now discovered. Thumblerock was charged with restoring the order of things.

He couldn't risk being seen on Earth by anyone other than Rosie. The connection between them was embedded in generations past. He hoped he'd convinced her enough to return for their second meeting tomorrow.

Sitting in an old rocking chair by a fire of leaping rainbow colours, Thumblerock said aloud, "I thought it went well. She seems a sensible, bright young thing. Just like her great-grandfather – though, always questions. I suppose I'll find out tomorrow."

Outside on the moon's surface, the freezing, faintly lit atmosphere blew the snow around violently. A death wish for anyone who dared to venture outside of this unusual habitation.

The dwelling looked like an Earth log cabin. It was constructed of large white tree trunk-shaped sections. The whole cabin shimmered with all the colours of a rainbow, just like Rosie's little silver box and the fire in the grate. Only this cabin existed here – nothing else that was identifiable as a lifeform. Thumblerock shivered with some apprehension. He hated these places, these desolate wastelands.

Thumblerock rose from his chair, walked over and stared out of the tiny window. Intermittent glimpses of starlight peeped through the driving snow. He felt homesick, and longed to walk in the sunshine of his home planet; with luck, he would soon have Rosie and Hattie with him. He returned to his chair by the fireside, put his feet up on an old stool and drifted away into a fitful sleep.

He was awoken some hours later by a hammering on the outside of the cabin walls. Lightning flashed outside like evil spirits duelling. There was no door; anything unlucky enough to be outside was unable to enter and unwelcome. Thumblerock pulled a blanket over himself and returned to his slumber trying to ignore the sounds. *Only a few more hours*, he thought, then a return to Earth for his next meeting with Rosie.

The sun rose to reveal another pleasant late summer morning on Earth. Rosie woke suddenly to the sound of a black bird shrieking in alarm outside her window. All the memories of the previous day flooded back into her mind. She played the events through, step by step, trying to understand the nature of the meeting with the Troll.

Reaching under the pillow for the small silver box, her stomach did a somersault. Was it a dream? Retrieving it, she shivered with that goosebump feeling and stared at it in wonder. The waves of colour, the tinkling bells and the static charge pricking her palm generated such a sense of wonder within her. She wasn't really worried anymore, just curious and eager to see how the next part of the puzzle would play out.

She threw on her clothes and ran downstairs. Hattie was hard on her heels, desperate to get to her food bowl.

"Outside first before breakfast," said Rosie. She opened the back door to let her out. Hattie bombed into the garden, chasing a few birds who were alarmed at the onrush of paws, teeth and a wagging tail.

Rosie filled up her bowl with some dog biscuits and put the kettle on for Grandma. She'd take her a cup of coffee and a slice of toast.

A little later, she sat at the breakfast table with a bowl of cereal looking out into the pretty garden. Hattie lay on the grass outside, rolling over and over, wriggling with effort to scratch her back.

Grandma came into the room and sat down.

"What's the plan today, Grandma?"

"Well," she said, "I thought we could walk into the village if you like. It looks like a nice day. We can pop into the café and have a hot chocolate. I've a little shopping to do and when we return, will you take Hattie for a walk again for me?"

"Of course, Grandma. I can do that, no problem."

So, it was settled; Rosie was going back to the woods that afternoon with Hattie, to meet the Troll again. She was feeling a little guilty not telling Grandma. However, she knew it was the right thing to do.

Back at the cabin, Thumblerock paced up and down waiting for the right time to journey back to Earth. It mustn't be too early, or too late. There was always a risk he could be seen – he wanted to avoid that at all costs. On the other hand, he didn't want to miss Rosie. That would be a disaster. He stood in front of the large fireplace, which still danced with vibrant flaming colours. He put his hand into his coat pocket and grasped a small silver box, then stepped straight into the flames.

In an instant, he was swept along a colour stream; he could see the Earth hurtling towards him. Within seconds, he could feel the touch of the cold, damp earth under his feet. *It must have been raining overnight,* he thought. A small stream of water flowed through the tunnel, making the ground soft and squelchy. He made his way towards the entrance, peering through the dim light.

As he approached the tunnel entrance, he could make out the silhouette of a stocky black shape, and a wagging tail. It was framed in the light of the tunnel opening and barking at him.

"Hello, Hattie," he said softly, and knelt to rub her head and chin. Hattie looked at him, then at his pocket. "Here you are, old girl, have a chew."

"Thanks," said Hattie, with an expectant hope that another one might appear.

"Is the coast clear? Can I go out without being seen?"

"No one around but Rosie," grumbled Hattie, and she turned and trotted out.

Rosie was standing on the bridge looking over. She saw Hattie come out, then breathed in sharply as Thumblerock strode out into the wood below.

"I still didn't know if it was all a dream," she said. "Here we are again, so it must be real."

"Oh, it's real enough," said Thumblerock. "How do you feel about coming down here so we can talk in private?" Hattie barked and grumbled.

"I expect that's Hattie telling me it's okay?"

"Yes, yes," said Thumblerock. "She said she'll keep a look out for us." Hattie scrambled back up to the bridge, sat down by Rosie and barked just once.

"Okay, Hattie, I get it, I'm going." Hattie grumbled again before lying down with her head between her paws.

Rosie picked her way down the steep path at the side of the bridge and stood in front of the Troll. He was a sight to behold. She stared up at him; he must have been two and a half metres tall. The duffel coat, the bright gold buttons, his sparkling green eyes smiling down at her. He took a step towards Rosie before bending down and holding out his hand.

"Can I introduce myself properly? I'm Thumblerock of Damianos, a planet in the Constellation of Taurus, and the star cluster of Pleadies."

Taking his enormous hand in hers and grinning, she said, "I'm Rosie of Earth, a planet to be found within the Orion Spur of the Milky Way galaxy." Thumblerock gave a small laugh and looked very impressed.

"Blimey," he said. "Your schooling must have improved enormously since your great-grandfather's days."

The young girl felt relieved; she could see that there was no malice in this Troll's eyes. In fact, being in his presence, she experienced a sense of calm and well-being. Thumblerock beckoned her inside the tunnel so they could talk in private. He didn't waste any time.

"Rosie, I need you and Hattie, of course, to travel back with me to my world? We need you to close a gate for us. I can't tell you much more at this stage, except that you are the only person on your whole world who can do this. It's the nature of the gate you see. It's operated by a genetic lock. The last time I came here, many years ago, was to ask your great-grandfather to open it."

"So now you want me to close it?" asked Rosie.

"Yes," said Thumblerock. "It's become a bit of an unexpected problem for us. Our ruling Council want to meet you. They can explain much better than I can. That's why I need you to come with me now."

"What about Grandma? She's expecting me home after our walk."

"Oh, yes, of course, please don't you worry about that. The way the gates work, I can get you back here at almost the same time as we leave."

"Is that time travel?" asked Rosie, looking a little confused.

"No, not really. Well, a little bit I guess, but in general it's all to do with travelling faster than the speed of light you see."

"How long will we be away?" she said.

"Oh, well probably not more than a few days I expect," said Thumblerock. Rosie took a step back and looked a little shocked.

"A few days, and then we can return here at the same time as we left?"

"Yes, said Thumblerock." She leant against the damp tunnel wall thinking.

"That's amazing. Will we be safe? Is it dangerous?"

"I'm here to make sure that no harm will come to you – on my honour as a representative of the planet Damianos," said Thumblerock. "I'm sorry, Rosie, I expect it's a bit of a muddle in your mind, but we need you. I wouldn't have come all this way to find you if it weren't terribly important."

"How do we get there? Is it something to do with this tunnel? Is there a magic train or something?" Rosie fired questions at the Troll.

"Do you have your motivator with you?" asked Thumblerock.

"What's a motivator?" she asked.

"It's a little silver box your grandma should have given you."

"Yes, oh yes," she said. "She gave it to me last night. It's wonderful. So that's what you call it, a motivator?"

"It's your train ticket so's to speak. It's genetically tied to you and your world. Only you can use it, as your great-grandfather did before you. You must always keep it safe.

Never lose it – it's important. It will help us to close the gate once you've returned home."

"I understand," she said. "I must go and check on Hattie. It will give me time to think."

"Yes, of course," said Thumblerock. "Take some time. When you're ready, come back into the tunnel and bring Hattie with you. I'll stay here for half an hour, then I must return with you, or without. I'll understand if you decide not to come back." He said that, but Rosie could see the apprehension behind his bright green eyes.

She looked at her watch, although it was too dark in the tunnel to see it properly. *I'll look when I get outside*, she thought, and turned and walked out. Rosie could hear him muttering in a slightly agitated state as she left the tunnel. She climbed back up the hill to the path, and found Hattie chewing grass and coughing again. Hattie turned to look at her, then ambled over and sat by her feet.

"What shall we do, Hattie?" Rosie knelt and rubbed the dog's head. "The Troll wants us to go with him to his world. It all sounds a bit scary." Hattie licked her hand and grumbled.

Rosie stood back up and walked up and down the path, just wondering. Hattie followed her back and forth. She thought about her great-grandad and the same decision he must have made. It all seemed a bit too much to take in. She had met a Troll in the woods, not far from Grandma's house. This Troll knew her great-grandad, and now he wanted her to accompany him on some kind of fantastic journey. Who wouldn't want to go if this were all true?

She played out the pieces of the story again and again in her mind. Her great-grandfather's request in his will. The beautiful silver box and his stories to his daughter, her grandma. It must be true. Should she now play her part and see where it led?

Rosie wasn't sure how long she'd been doing this, when she suddenly remembered that she should have looked at her watch when leaving the tunnel.

"Quick, Hattie, we have to go. I hope we're not too late!"

She ran back up the path in a panic, with Hattie right behind her, down the side of the tunnel and into the dark entrance. It wasn't so dark this time. Ahead of her, a beautiful display of flaming colours enveloped the enormous figure of the Troll and there was the distant sound of ringing bells. She saw Thumblerock's face turn towards her. He quickly stepped backwards out of the flames and walked towards them.

"Oh, I thought you'd gone home," he said. "I waited well over the half hour we agreed."

"I'm sorry," said Rosie, breathing deeply after her run. "We nearly missed you. We want to come," she heard herself say. "If we can help, we will." Hattie barked, and asked Thumblerock for a biscuit, which he gladly obliged. "You will get us home as promised, so Grandma won't worry?"

"I made the same promise to your great-grandfather, those many years ago. You'll be back in time for your tea, and your grandma will be none the wiser. Don't you worry."

"How do we do this then, Thumblerock? Can I call you Rocky, too? It's much easier to say."

"Yes, yes, of course you can. Now stand by me, and I'll kneel by Hattie with my arm around her. Have you got your little box?"

Rosie searched in her coat pocket and pulled out the little silver box. It immediately began to ring and radiate a rainbow.

"Clasp it in the palm of your hand, as I've done with mine." He looped his arm through hers, and Rosie heard him say something softly which she couldn't quite catch.

"Will it hurt?" she asked, alarmed, but the sound of her voice disappeared in a whirl of colour and ringing bells. It was like being on a fair ride with neon lights flashing by your vision. She looked behind her to see the Earth disappearing, and then ahead a small white globe was rushing madly towards them.

The next moment she was stood in a large fireplace, in some sort of a cabin, with the sound of wind and snow beating hard against a tiny window.

"Come out of there now, Rosie. You might feel a little dizzy for a minute. Take a seat here by the fire."

She walked out with Hattie and looked back. The fireplace immediately erupted with leaping flames of many colours, radiating warmth all around the cabin. Hattie promptly lay down on a rug in front of it and fell asleep.

"Will she be all right, Rocky?"

"She'll be fine. As a small animal, it takes a little more out of them. She'll sleep it off, then be right as snow." Rosie laughed.

"As right as *snow*? It's as right as rain!"

"Is it?" he said. "I'm sure Michael used to say that. He was pulling my leg, wasn't he? Well, it doesn't matter. How do you feel now?"

"I'm okay. I just feel a little dizzy – that was quite a ride. Where are we?" Rosie went over to the small window, put her hands around her eyes to block out the cabin lights and peered outside.

"We're on a small moon, about half the distance between our two worlds. We can't travel the whole way at once, you see, as it's tough on the body. We'll both need some rest before we complete the journey." Rosie could just about see some distant stars twinkling amongst the driving snow.

Suddenly, a loud bang echoed around the cabin, as if someone or something had struck the outside. Rosie nearly jumped out of her skin.

"What was that?" she shrieked.

"Oh, never you mind. What's outside can't get in here, so just try to ignore it."

Rosie retreated from the window and returned to her seat by the fire. She was visibly shaken. Thumblerock brought her a hot drink.

"Here," he said, "have this. It will calm your nerves and help you to sleep. I told you that you'd be safe with me, and I meant it. Whatever exists on any world can sometimes seem pleasant or unpleasant – it depends on your point of view. Just bear it no mind; it's not part of our story."

Staring at the little window, Rosie felt a little comforted by his words, but not much. He came over and sat down in a chair next to her. They both drank the hot, sweet beverage. She felt herself drifting away and vaguely remembered Thumblerock placing a blanket over her and the same for Hattie, who was now snoring loudly.

Thumblerock retook his seat and stared into the flames. An occasional bang from outside interrupted his thoughts. He pulled a blanket over himself and joined them in slumber.

Chapter 3 One Small Step

Rosie opened her eyes; she saw Hattie tucking into a bowl of something tasty. The dog turned her head to say hello, then continued with her meal. Thumblerock came over with a small, hammered metal plate and handed it to Rosie.

"Here you are – nothing special mind, just something to fill you up before we set off again."

"Thanks," said Rosie. "How long have we been sleeping?"

"Oh, about five or six hours I expect. It's hard to tell here with no sunlight as a guide. We've been here quite long enough, though."

She looked at the small plate, which contained what looked like a salad. She picked some up and put it into her mouth. The taste didn't disappoint. Sweet, crispy and crunchy, with a fabulous colourful flavour. A bit like her whole experience so far with Thumblerock. Everything was either wildly colourful and happy or, as she looked towards the little window, cold, dark and ominous. She would be glad to leave this place.

Thumblerock was buzzing about tidying and putting everything away in hidden cupboards and drawers. He seemed much happier, as though a weight had been lifted from his shoulders. Rosie and Hattie were with him, and they were about to travel back to his home world.

"My dearest new companions, it's time we left here. It will be my privilege to introduce you to my world." He beckoned them towards him. They took up the same positions in the fireplace. "You have your motivator, Rosie?"

"Yes, I do." Her fingers were wrapped tightly around the little silver box. She could feel the tingling and the expectation in her stomach.

Thumblerock said softly, "Damianos." Fireworks suddenly erupted all around them. They hurtled away from the strange dark moon and forward towards a colourful glowing orb, approaching them at a terrific speed.

They arrived somewhere in total darkness. Within a few seconds, Rosie became aware of a colourful flowing light within the roof, which revealed what looked like the inside of a tree. Ahead were a few steps.

"Follow me," he said, and began to climb upward. He pushed open an old wooden door and stepped out into an amazing bright and colourful wooded glade.

Rosie stumbled out behind him. She felt as though she'd been slapped in the face. The smell was overwhelming. A sweet fragrance of meadow flowers, grass, honey – and what else was it, lime or tangerine?

She sat down immediately, right next to Hattie, who was obviously reacting in the same way. The dog's nose went into overdrive, sniffing the air. She lay down full stretch on the sweet grass and put her head down flat between her front paws. She made a small squeaking noise, as if a mild panic were setting in.

Thumblerock came over and gave Hattie something to chew from his pocket. Rosie looked at him blankly, still unable to communicate.

"Just relax and take some slow steady breaths in and out. Your body will adjust to the atmosphere; it may take a few minutes. Your brain is trying to cope with an information overload. It's the increased oxygen level you see. It's a lot higher than your body is used to processing on your world."

"It's the smells," blurted out Rosie. "It's overwhelming." She was beginning to regain some composure. Hattie got up and began to wander slowly between the plants and trees. "She seems all right now. Can I have one of those chews you gave her?"

"You'll be fine in a few minutes. I gave something to Hattie. She has more heightened senses than you, so I needed to calm her. It would have been too much for her to cope with all at once."

"So, this is Damianos?" said Rosie.

"Yes, yes," said Thumblerock. "My world, and mighty proud I am to live here."

"I can see why," she spluttered. "It seems beautiful and peaceful – at least this part anyway. Is it all like this?"

"Well, yes, I suppose it is. We have villages, farms and small settlements, a number of towns, but only one Central Domain. I guess you would call it a city on your world. We don't have any cars, polluting machines or large factories. Everything is in balance, and that's how we like it. That's why you are here in a way; our ruling Council want to talk with you about Earth."

"Oh," said Rosie, looking a bit pensive. "I don't know if I can help them with that. I'm just a young girl remember."

"Well, they'll want to talk with you, about closing the gate. You're special to us, Rosie, which is why we needed you to come here."

"I know, you've said that a number of times. I still don't really know what that means?"

"Don't be too concerned about that now – all will be explained in good time. First, would you like to come to our farm and meet my mate and all our friends who live with us?"

"Of course, I'd love to."

As Rosie recovered, Thumblerock led them down a cinder track towards a cabin. It was constructed in a similar way to the one on the dark moon. It was made of the same white logs with two large doors. He pulled at a handle and swung one of them open. Inside were four carriages, all lined up, just like old Wild West stagecoaches on Earth.

They were beautifully decorated with pastel-coloured panels and large glass windows. As he opened the door of one, some steps silently dropped down.

"Up you go."

Hattie jumped straight in and sat in a corner by a window. Rosie followed and took the seat next to her. The carriage had soft comfy red seats and was decorated with green and red curtains that were pulled back with a gold cord.

Thumblerock climbed in and sat down opposite them. He took his motivator out of his pocket, opened a panel in the carriage wall and pushed the little box into a slot, with a satisfying pop. He then whispered something Rosie couldn't quite hear, and the carriage began to move slowly out of the cabin and down towards a leafy lane, heading away between the trees. The ride was beautifully smooth, as though they were gliding on air.

"Tell me a little more about the silver boxes, the motivators, and how they work?" she asked.

"All right," he said. "We've been fortunate on this world. The mineral contained within the silver box is an amazing power source. It was discovered here many generations ago. It's enabled us to power just about everything. It doesn't pollute and it helps us all to live in balance with nature. I guess the closest comparison to it on your world would be nuclear power, although it doesn't create the pollution issues you have."

"It all sounds so perfect," said Rosie. She was feeling a little ashamed of society on Earth.

"We do have one minor drawback," said Thumblerock. "Being in close contact with the mineral over time is addictive. It doesn't really harm; it's just that we can't be parted from it for any significant length of time without suffering withdrawal symptoms. Don't worry yourself, though; the exposure takes many years to create the addiction. As a society, we decided the drawbacks were well worth the benefits. No pollutants or the need to burn carbon-based materials for power generation."

"We are trying," said Rosie. "There's lots of people on our world who want to change the way we live. It's especially important for the young people, the environment I mean, and all the animals."

"I know, Rosie, I know." Thumblerock stretched his feet across the seat and closed his eyes. Rosie stared out of the window trying to enjoy the lovely views from the coach windows. She felt a little troubled by the conversation.

Occasionally, a cart came the other way. Rosie waved at the occupants who waved back. She could see that they were a little surprised by her appearance; they smiled curiously at her. They all seemed to be Trolls. Why was she surprised? This was their world.

Small dwellings and ploughed fields drifted past. She could also see some animals in the fields, which looked familiar. They all seemed much larger. In general, they seemed the same as on the Earth, which she found surprising. The best way to describe what she was seeing was like an artist's oil painting. Everything seemed bigger and brighter with more vivid colours, as though bursting with life.

An hour or so must have passed before Thumblerock stirred from his slumber. "Not far now," he said suddenly, looking out of the window.

"Oh," said Rosie. "Your mate – can you tell me about her? I'm ashamed to say, I haven't asked you anything about your life."

"Not to worry," he said. "It's been a lot for you to come to terms with. My mate's name is Alannah. She is so beautiful; I know I'm a lucky Troll. We live on a farm, as do many of us. We grow our own food and look after the other animals in the area. They are our friends and companions. As you know, we can talk with each other, but we don't eat each other." Once again, Rosie was stung with Thumblerock's last comment.

"I apologise once again for my world," she said. "We seem to do the opposite; you must think we are barbarians."

"No, no, Rosie, you misunderstand me. I apologise if I've offended you. I'm not here to judge. Your world and the life on it have evolved in a different way. Please don't be hard on yourselves. There are plenty of worlds out there that are dark, evil places, somewhere none of us would want to live. For us, a common language has been the key to our development. After all, you wouldn't want to eat a horse you shared a conversation with the previous evening, would you?"

"I guess not," said Rosie.

"It didn't happen all at once, though. Many generations passed following the discovery of the crystal. Our exposure to it over time stimulated something within our genetic make-up. It gave us all the ability to start communicating with each other. The exposure to the crystal has infiltrated the evolution of all the species on our planet."

"I wish I could talk with the animals?" said Rosie. "I'd love to hear more about what Hattie says to you."

"Oh yes, I'll let you know. She doesn't say much, though, only if she thinks it's worth saying I expect."

"I'm sure she'll love it here," she said.

At that, Hattie grumbled, to which Thumblerock laughed. "She just said as long as there's plenty of biscuits!" Rosie smiled. He suddenly pointed away in the distance. "That's our home."

She followed his gaze, and saw an old windmill, with its sails slowly turning in the breeze behind some trees. "You use wind power as well? Oh, it's so beautiful."

"Oh yes. Well, why not. It's there, and it's a free gift."

"We have them, too, all standing together. We call them wind farms," she said. "Although, these old-style windmills are generally just for people to live in. They're rarely used for their original purpose."

"Ahh, that's a shame," he said. "Very useful for the farms they are."

They turned off the main route onto a path leading up towards Thumblerock's farm. They soon rolled into a small courtyard with buildings on three sides, one of them being the windmill. As a sail swooped past a door, a figure ran out towards them. Rosie guessed it must be Alannah.

Thumblerock jumped down from the carriage and emotionally embraced his mate. Hattie followed and sat down by them. She offered her paw to the female Troll. Alannah knelt down, took her paw, lay a hand on her head and said something. Hattie barked, and then scurried off before disappearing through another door.

Rosie climbed carefully down from the carriage. It was quite a drop. She stood in front of Thumblerock and his mate.

"Hello, Rosie," said Alannah. "I'm pleased you have both arrived here safely. I know you've come a long way. I've prepared some food. You must be hungry?"

Rosie was quite stunned by Alannah's appearance. Although tall and obviously a Troll, she had a beautiful soft kind face, long black curly hair and the same fluorescent green eyes. She wore tight black moleskin-type trousers to just below her knees, a pair of fine black leather square-ended boots with white socks rolled over the top, a white blouse with puffed sleeves and a black leather waistcoat.

"Thank you," said Rosie. "I'm quite tired, and a little overwhelmed by the beauty of your world. I hope I can be of service to you all. Although, I'm not exactly sure why I'm here."

"Spend a few days with us so you can recover your strength. We'll tell you as much as we know. You mustn't fret; you are our guest in our home. We want you to enjoy your stay with us."

The pair of them towered over Rosie. She knew Thumblerock was tall, but his mate was of equal height, somewhere around two and a half metres, she guessed.

"Come with me," said Alannah. "Rocky has a few things to do and he must return the carriage to the locus, a little way down the trail." She then said to Thumblerock, "Take Quizzical with you. She wants to talk to you anyway."

"Who's Quizzical?" asked Rosie.

"She's one of the horses that lives here with us on the farm. She has some business to discuss with Rocky. She can give him a ride home after he's dropped the carriage. They won't be long."

Rosie followed Alannah into the farmhouse kitchen. How was she ever going to tell anyone on Earth about all of this? She realised she couldn't – no one would believe it anyway. *I suppose*, she thought, *that's why great-grandad told his magical stories*. She smiled to herself. *Well, I can do the same I expect. At least I will have the satisfaction of knowing it's all true.*

The farmhouse kitchen was just amazing – just what you would expect to find in a Victorian farmhouse kitchen on Earth. A large, knotted table with benches each side, a wooden dresser with pots, pans and utensils. A large metal oven with a rainbow fire burning behind the glass doors and pans steaming on the top plates. At the end of the kitchen, a large fireplace with a rainbow fire in the hearth, a few rocking chairs, and a black Labrador fast asleep in front of it.

"I hope you don't mind," said Alannah. "I told Hattie to go straight in, as I'd put some food out for her."

"I expect she's in heaven," said Rosie.

"Do you have your motivator?" asked Alannah.

"I do." Rosie took it out of her pocket.

"We'll keep it in a cradle for you if you don't mind? Has Rocky warned you of the side effects?"

"Yes."

"Well, better for your sake if you don't have it with you all the time. We want you to have as little exposure as possible." Alannah took the silver box from Rosie and clicked it into a slot in a cabinet on the wall, then closed the door. Rosie noticed another one already sitting in place next to it, just like a fuse box on Earth.

"Does that one provide the power for the farm?" asked Rosie.

"Yes, it does," said Alannah, a little surprised. "That's mine, and there's another few spaces for Rocky's, or if we have visitors. With all those motivators, it's best to have them shielded in the cabinet."

"I understand," said Rosie. "You call him Rocky as well, like my great-grandad?"

"Yes, I do. Thumblerock is such a mouthful, and he loves the name. It's become an important part of his life history. We all remember your great-grandad. He was a lovely boy, so full of life."

"You knew him, then?" asked Rosie.

"Yes, he came here as you have now, and I expect you are about the same age." Rosie looked a little puzzled.

"If we assume great-grandad died about twenty-five years ago at fifty-six years old, which is not old on Earth, it still doesn't make sense to me. How long do you all live?"

"Well," said Alannah, "we do have a longer lifespan than you. Some of us live to be over two hundred years old. Our years are broadly the same as your time span on Earth. You must also remember though, you travelled here faster than the speed of light, which also complicates my answer. The best way to think about it is, we all live in our own time – it's only the motivators that can join us together in the here and now."

Alannah looked a little sad as she turned away from Rosie. The memories of their time with Michael came flooding back to her mind.

"Have a seat by the fire, and I'll bring you some soup."

Rosie took off her coat and hung it on a hook by the door, then went across to the rocking chairs. She sat down in a huge chair next to Hattie. She watched Alannah move gracefully around the kitchen. She brought across a large, round mug of soup for Rosie. It was thick and tasty; each mouthful contained some soft spicy vegetable. It was the best soup she'd ever tasted – even Grandma's came second to this.

Chapter 4 All Together Now

Alannah sat down beside Rosie and took her hand in hers. "The Council have asked you to come here because you are special, and only you can close the gate between our worlds. It's your motivator which keeps the door open."

"I understand some of this," said Rosie. "From what Rocky has said, is it just the gate to Earth which must be closed?"

"It is, yes. I'm afraid I don't have all the answers for you," said Alannah, "which is why we're going to take you to see the Council. They want to talk to you to explain why the gate on Earth must be closed." Rosie looked a little concerned.

"Does that mean I will never be able to come back here again?"

"I just don't know the answer to that question. It's complicated," replied Alannah.

Rosie smiled faintly. "I'm looking forward to seeing more of your world whilst I'm here, though," she said, trying not to look as sad as she was feeling.

"We have a few days before you leave for the Council meeting," said Alannah. "We want you to enjoy your time discovering the farm and finding out how we live."

Thumblerock came into the kitchen, placed his motivator in the cupboard and served himself some soup. He came and sat with them in front of the fire. He could sense the mood, so didn't say anything for a little while.

"How's Quizzical?" asked Rosie.

"Oh fine, fine," he said. "She's a sensible old soul."

"I just think it's the best thing that you are able to speak with the animals. I can't quite imagine how it all works. It's just amazing," said Rosie.

"It's just a different way of living with each other than you are used to," he said. "It can get a bit complicated sometimes when all have to have their say."

Rosie chuckled. "I bet it is."

"I thought I'd take you on a tour of some of the farm in the morning," said Alannah. "After we've all rested, and in the afternoon, would you like to come with us to the market?"

"Sounds wonderful," said Rosie.

"Good, good," said Thumblerock. "Well, I'm beat," he grumbled. "I need my bed."

Hattie got up, stretched and looked at each of them in turn before barking and walking to the door.

"Okay, Hattie," said Rosie. "I know what that means. You want to go out before bed. Can I let her out?"

"I'll take her out with me," said Thumblerock. "I need to settle the hens and stop the mill – the wind is blowing up." He walked to the door and disappeared outside with Hattie.

"Take off your boots and put them near the fire," said Alannah. "I'll show you to the room we've prepared for you. There's a surprise in there which has been waiting for you, for about seventy years if my maths is correct."

Rosie followed her through a door and along a corridor with rooms on both sides before turning up a flight of stairs. At the top was a square landing with four doors opposite each other.

"This one is for you," said Alannah, as she swung the door open.

Once again it was rustic, quaint and pretty, with drapes pulled back at a little cottage window. There was a wooden dressing table, some drawers, and a solid bed on the back wall looking across towards the window.

After walking in and looking out into the farmyard below, she could see Thumblerock and Hattie lit up by colourful lanterns. Both were sat on bales of straw, talking! They looked up. Thumblerock waved, and Hattie barked.

It's like being in a fairy tale, thought Rosie to herself. *I still can't quite believe it.*

"There's a bathroom across the hall," said Alannah. "When you're settled, there's a message for you in the drawer of the dressing table. Have a well-earned rest – you deserve it. You're so brave, just like your great-grandfather Michael." Alannah retreated, leaving Rosie to herself.

She took off her clothes and put on the beautiful cotton nightshirt that had been laid out on the bed. She crossed to the bathroom and washed in the bowl. She pumped a handle for a smooth flow of warm water. It made her smile. Everything seemed so manual, although she could tell it was all obviously backed up by the silent power of the motivators.

Upon returning to her room, she went to the drawer of the dressing table. Inside was a piece of parchment rolled up with a red ribbon tied around it. She carefully untied the ribbon and smoothed out the parchment. Rosie then crossed to the bed, where a lantern on the wall was throwing a colourful warm light, enough to read by, and started to read the beautifully written script.

Hello great-grandson or great-granddaughter, My name is Mike, your great-grandfather, which is a bit weird. If all goes well, you may have come to this world with Thumblerock. I know this is all a lot to take in – and believe me, I thought I'd been hit on the head by a Leprechaun!

Rosie smiled, and was surprised to feel a tear running down her cheek. She continued to read.

I was brought here to open the gate, and find out about this wonderful world and others we are all connected to. I just wanted to help you understand that all you see is real. Thumblerock and Alannah made me feel so welcome, even though Quizzical and myself got up to some mischief. It was all her fault. I'll say no more about that. What I want to say is, don't waste time worrying about it. Just enjoy your time here, and don't forget to write to your great-grandson or great-granddaughter before you leave. They will be feeling as confused as you and I when we arrived!
Michael

Rosie put down the letter and sat on her bed thinking about the whole experience so far. She could tell that Michael had really enjoyed his stay here. He didn't seem to have been burdened with such an onerous task. What were the implications of closing the gate? Would she be writing her note to her great-grandchildren when she was due to leave? It didn't seem so. She just couldn't help this feeling of a distant sadness, wrapping ever so slowly around her.

"Oh, stop fretting, Rosie," she said to herself. "Enjoy the moment, as Michael said in his letter."

She climbed between the lovely freshly laundered sheets; it was just like being back at Grandma's. She was tired. It had been an unusual day. She put her head on the pillow and drifted off into a deep sleep.

When she awoke, the sun was shining brightly through a crack in the curtains. She could hear the windmill sails spinning outside, with a faint *whoosh* every few seconds. A horse was trotting nearby, and she could hear voices below, just out of range to hear any words.

She leapt out of bed, feeling quite refreshed and alive, looking forward to her first day on the farm. The sadness of the previous evening had retreated. *Today is a new day*, she said to herself. *Let's make the most of it*.

Alannah had obviously been into the room earlier and left some lovely soft socks, a checked shirt, and a pair of dungarees with leather on the inside of the legs. She supposed for horse riding. *How exciting*, she thought.

She ran to the bathroom, washed, then charged downstairs to the kitchen. Alannah was just coming through the door from the yard with a basket full of eggs.

"Hello, Alannah," said Rosie, a little shyly.

"Hello, Rosie, I hope you slept well. Those dungarees fit you perfectly. A neighbour of ours gave them to me. They were her daughter's, but she grew out of them some time ago."

"They do," said Rosie excitedly. "Are they for horse riding?"

"Yes, is that okay?" asked Alannah. "I thought I'd show you the farm on horseback. It's just too far to walk around. If you still want to, you can accompany us to the market this afternoon?"

Rosie thought she was dreaming again, for a second time. She managed to compose herself. "That sounds wonderful. I can't imagine how I could plan a better day."

"Oh, that's good. I wasn't sure if you liked horse riding. Sit down at the table, and I'll get you some breakfast. I have some eggs and fresh bread?"

"Sounds lovely." Within a few minutes, Rosie was tucking into a vegetable omelette, a crusty roll with some fruit jam and a glass of fresh milk. When she had finished her meal, she asked, "Where's Hattie?"

"Oh, I'm sorry. She left early with Rocky. She wanted to wait for you. When Rocky asked her to accompany him on some business at a neighbouring farm, she was just too eager to be out. I hope you don't mind. I told her I'd explain when you came down."

"No that's fine," said Rosie. "It's all new to her, too. I don't blame her. To be able to talk to you and the other animals here, it must be just amazing for her."

"She's a clever dog," said Alannah. "Rocky is quite taken with her and is enjoying her company. You'll see her this afternoon."

"Okay," said Rosie, feeling a little jealous, but it was only a passing thought.

Once breakfast was over, the two of them put on a light cotton jacket from a rail by the back door. Of course, there was one to fit Rosie perfectly. Alannah also passed her a straw boater-style hat with a yellow ribbon tied around it.

"I don't want you catching too much starlight here. Your body will take a few days to adjust."

"Starlight," said Rosie. "That's a lovely description. It makes sense, though." Alannah smiled, and they left the kitchen to head for the stable.

"I've spoken with Quizzical and the other horses," said Alannah. "They're looking forward to meeting you. Quizzical said she would be honoured to carry you on our expedition today."

Rosie beamed. "That's the horse Rocky was with last night, and Michael talked about in his letter when he was here?"

"Yes, they were quite a pair – couldn't separate them." Alannah laughed. "She was upset when Rocky told her of his passing. It wasn't so long ago he was here, in our time frame."

"Oh," said Rosie. "I hope she likes me too?"

"Of course she will. She'll see the resemblance immediately, as we have."

Alannah pushed open the large stable door, which creaked on its hinges. Inside, several enormous, beautiful horses stood together around a stone trough. They were chewing straw whilst looking as though having a discussion. They all turned around as Alannah and Rosie walked in.

"Good morning," said Alannah. She bowed slightly; the horses returned the gesture. "May I present Rosie, from Earth. The great-granddaughter of Michael, who came to visit us a time ago."

One large silky black horse with a white flash on her nose replied directly to Alannah, although Rosie only heard neighing. The horse walked slowly up to Rosie and bowed her head ever so slightly. Rosie repeated the gesture respectfully.

She was a magnificent beast, probably at least eighteen or twenty hands in Earth measurement, and she towered above Rosie.

"This is Quizzical," said Alannah. "She is pleased to meet the granddaughter of Michael. He was a particular friend of hers, and she is so sorry she will never see him again." Rosie took a step towards the horse and gently placed her hand on the side of her neck.

"I never met him, Quizzical. I can only imagine your sadness." Rosie thought she saw a tear in the corner of Quizzical's eye, and felt herself welling up. Quizzical shook her head softly, then nuzzled her nose into Rosie's hair. "She understands me?"

"She does," said Alannah. The horse said something to Alannah, who smiled. "She says she can see a family resemblance, although you are much better looking than Michael was." Rosie laughed.

Rosie, Alannah, Quizzical and another female horse called Ceres collected in the yard as they prepared to set off for the farm tour. Alannah gave Rosie a small backpack, which contained a flask of cold water and the largest apple she had ever seen. She helped her up into the saddle. Rosie looked around from this lofty position, almost dizzy with excitement, as well as a slight sense of acrophobia – she was so far from the ground on this enormous horse. Alannah mounted Ceres, spoke softly and they all set off at a gentle pace.

"I can't find the reins?" Rosie suddenly shouted to Alannah.

Ceres stopped and turned her head. "We don't need them here," said Alannah. "We all know where we are going. The horses are taking us, not the other way around. To hold on, use the ring on the front of the saddle."

"Of course," said Rosie. "How foolish of me. Please don't be offended, Quizzical, I meant no disrespect." The horses both whinnied, and Alannah smiled.

"No offence taken; they think it's rather funny."

They continued out of the yard at a gentle walk and past a collection of low-level buildings, which housed several other animals. They all seemed to be going about their business, nodding respectfully as they walked past.

"Alannah," said Rosie. "Can you explain to me how the farm works, for all the animals and yourselves?"

"Well," she replied, "we all live here, in the accommodation that suits us. Thumblerock and I live in the farmhouse, and the animals of the farm in their respective barns, stables or enclosures, as is their choice. It operates as a type of collective I suppose. We all help each other to run the farm and grow the food we need to thrive. We also trade our excess produce and services within the community, as you will see this afternoon."

"It all sounds so refreshingly simple," said Rosie. "We have similar collective arrangements in some countries on our world, but it never seems to work. People just don't seem to get on with each other as you do here."

"Ah, Rosie," said Alannah, "I understand your world is different, as are the other worlds in the galaxy. Who can say which system is best? We all make sacrifices, and especially here on Damianos. We have to consider the feelings of all the creatures who inhabit our world."

"I can see how that could complicate matters," said Rosie.

They picked up the pace to a gentle trot as they left the farm behind and followed a track between enormous fields. Tall crops like corn and barley were swaying in the breeze. Some pigs and a few horses were busily working amongst them.

"What are they doing?" asked Rosie.

Alannah pointed out each animal and identified their roles. The pigs were turning the soil between the rows of crops, keeping the lanes clear of weeds. Large hedgehogs followed snapping up insects and bugs, which were disturbed by the pigs. The horses were pulling carts back and forth to and from the agricultural machinery with harvested fruits and cereals.

"It's amazing," said Rosie. "A real community effort."

They came to the end of the track and approached a stream with the sound of a powerful waterfall somewhere in the distance. They clopped over a wooden bridge and headed into a shaded forest lane. Birds flittered here and there conducting their own business.

"Alannah," said Rosie, "how far does the communication between you and all the animals go? The birds, for instance, do they talk?"

"They do in their own way. There are some animals who don't form part of the community as such. They just live their lives as they would on your world. The difference being that we know when they need help, as they can tell us. We can then assist with shelter in bad weather or provide food if they are hungry through no fault of their own."

"I see," said Rosie. She was thinking of hundreds of other questions.

Before she could ask another, Alannah suddenly said, "Can you hear the waterfall? It's just around this corner."

As they rounded a copse of trees, they came to the edge of a large shimmering plunge pool. The waterfall just up ahead filled the air with a fine rainbow mist arising from the torrent, which thundered over a narrow gorge. It must have been about four metres high.

Rosie could spot fish torpedoing out of the water at an angle and floating up and over the waterfall beyond. The fish were pulling back their fins to create an almost circular wing.

"Wow!" she exclaimed. "That's amazing."

"They've come up from the lake and are heading for their spawning grounds," said Alannah.

Just then, a brightly coloured bird similar to a kingfisher on Earth, though much larger, shot out from the trees and grabbed a fish in mid-air. It was quite a spectacle.

"That's bad luck for the fish." Rosie laughed.

Alannah smiled and said, "Follow me. My brother lives in this wood. He's a carpenter. His home is just a little further down the lane."

Rosie smiled and asked, "What's his name?"

"He's known as Croaken. He tends to be a little grumpy, but take no notice – he has a good heart."

"Sounds like my grandad," said Rosie.

In the distance, she could hear the buzzing of equipment, like a chainsaw back home. Within a few minutes, they walked into a clearing with a large barn, some fencing and piles of wood stacked neatly around. Inside the barn, she could see a large Troll cutting wood on a long bench. Cartwheels and part finished farm equipment hung all around the walls.

The horses stopped just outside the barn, and Alannah dropped down gracefully to the ground. She walked over to Rosie and helped her down from Quizzical.

Alannah nodded at the horses, and they strode away slowly to find something to eat. Rosie and Alannah walked towards the barn. The Troll looked up and waved, stretched over his equipment and knocked off a large switch. The rotating saw started to reduce speed and quieten. Rosie could see the box on the wall with his motivator plugged in and glowing colourfully.

"If you've come for the farm cart, you're early. Lucky, though – it's ready and round the back. Who's this then, another one of Rocky's waifs?"

"Hello, Croaken," said Rosie before Alannah answered. "My name is Rosie, I'm visiting from Earth, and I'm pleased to meet you."

"Well, I'll be a rat's whisker," said Croaken. "You must be related to that other young fellow. Mike, was it? Caused me no end of bother. Never mind," he said. "I'm pleased to meet you as well, I hope." He grinned a little scarily.

He was enormous, probably another ten centimetres taller than Thumblerock, with jet black unruly hair tied back with a headband. There was a family resemblance to Alannah, but he was not attractive in any way. He had big shining green eyes, black eyebrows and a large nose. He wore moleskin trousers, big boots and a thick linen shirt opened all the way down to his trousers, exposing his hairy chest.

"Apologies," he said to Rosie and Alannah. He could see them both staring at him. "It's hot work." He began doing up a few shirt buttons. Come on into the house and have a drink if you like – I need one."

Alannah grinned at Rosie, and she smiled back, trying not to giggle. They followed him around the side of the barn towards a small cottage. Rosie ran to keep up with his huge strides.

He threw the door open, then turned and beckoned them in. "Come on, come on, I haven't got all day."

"Croaken, be civil," said Alannah. "You have a guest. I'm showing Rosie the farm, and as we were passing, I thought it would be nice for her to meet my big brother. If you're too busy, we will be on our way."

"No offence meant," said Croaken to Rosie. "It's my sister you see – she tends to get a bit touchy."

Rosie laughed, and they all grinned at each other, Alannah a little pensively.

"Have a seat." Croaken pointed to the bench in the middle of the kitchen. This was also surrounded by things hanging around the walls, pans and hooks with all sorts of kitchen or work implements that Rosie didn't recognise. "Hear you are." He produced a jug full of water with lemons floating in it, and then went to fetch some glasses. He sloppily poured out a glass for each of them, and they drank in silence for a few moments. It was sweet and sharp at the same time but refreshing. "So, are you staying all summer?" Croaken asked Rosie.

"I don't expect so," answered Rosie, glancing at Alannah. "I'm on an errand for Thumblerock. He's asked me to come and help to close the gate."

"Ahh," said Croaken. He looked a little embarrassed at what to say next. He obviously understood the implication of this statement. Something Rosie was still pretty much in the dark about. Alannah jumped in to ease the tension.

"Yes, Rosie is spending a day or two with us before she goes to meet the Council."

"Ugh, the Council. Wow, well that sounds like fun," said Croaken in a sarcastic manner.

"I understand there's an important part to my visit which worries me," said Rosie. "I don't fully understand what's expected of me. I'm trying not to think too much about it. Your world, it's just so beautiful."

Croaken smiled at Rosie with his big eyes. He stretched over and took her hand in his enormous fingers. "I think your world should be proud of sending such a special ambassador to help us all."

Rosie looked across the table at the two Trolls. "I need to know soon what this all means. I know you are all protecting me from something to do with this gate. I really can't imagine what it is?"

"Soon enough you will meet the Council," said Alannah. "They will explain everything in a much better way than we can. It's because you are so bright and special that you are here representing your world." There was now see a small tear in Alannah's eye, just beginning to creep down her cheek.

The young girl smiled to break the tension. "I'm trying not to worry, Alannah; you have all been so kind to me. Being here, it's just awesome."

"Awesome," said Croaken. "Not heard that word before."

"Yes, it just means fantastic or brilliant or cool."

"Cool," said Croaken, laughing. "I need to write these down and surprise my friends the next time we meet. I can tell them my new friend Rosie from Earth thinks I'm awesome and cool." Alannah laughed and punched her brother on the arm.

"Come on, Rosie, we must go. Can I take the cart back with us, then?" Alannah directed her question to Croaken.

"Yes, it's ready," he replied. "Will Quizzical and Ceres pull it? Better ask them."

"Oh, I'm sure they won't mind – it's not far. I'll go and speak with them now." Alannah walked out of the kitchen and headed for the horses.

"Follow me," said Croaken to Rosie. They turned out of the cottage and headed around the corner of the barn.

A large cart painted green and gold, with a soft leather bench seat, stood in front of them.

"Here you are, Rosie. I'll lift you up." Croaken helped her onto the seat. "I've just repaired this; a wheel was broken."

"Does this not work with the motivator?" Rosie asked Croaken.

"No, not this one. It's just used on the farm to move supplies around. The horses and the other large beasts can just use it on their own, without our help. They can't use the motivators, you see."

"Of course," said Rosie. "I didn't think of that."

"It's just us lazy old Trolls who have the motivators. That reminds me, I need to crack on and get a few things finished for customers today."

"It's been lovely to meet you," said Rosie.

"My pleasure," said Croaken. "Don't let those Council Trolls worry you either. I'm sure you're a match for them."

"I won't," she said, and waved to him as he walked back to his barn.

Quizzical and Ceres came around the corner and nodded at Rosie. They both approached the front of the cart and ducked their heads in between a rigid leather framework attached to the front. This settled neatly over their shoulders and allowed them to pull the cart slowly around the side of the barn. Once again, Rosie was amazed at the simplicity of the process, and said "cool" under her breath.

Alannah was speaking with her brother, so the horses stopped a few yards away. She hugged him, then walked towards the cart, climbed up and joined Rosie on the bench seat. She spoke to the horses, and they pulled slowly away back up the track. They all waved as Croaken disappeared into his barn. Shortly afterwards, Rosie could hear the machinery starting up again.

"We'll return directly to the farm now, Rosie. I could show you the other side to the north, but we are a little short of time for the market this afternoon. Perhaps you can go out again with Quizzical tomorrow if you like?" Rosie smiled and nodded but didn't reply.

The horses pulled the cart effortlessly back through the forest, over the stream and up through the fields towards the farm buildings.

Alannah sat in a reflective mood, occasionally smiling at Rosie and pointing out various things to see.

Rosie enjoyed the scenery, the warmth of the planet's star in the bright blue sky and the noise of the horses in what she assumed was deep conversation. She wondered if the horses at home talked with each other the same way. *If so, what must they think of humanity? What about all the other animals on the Earth? As the dominant species, we just don't seem to consider their potential intelligence or how effectively they communicate with each other,* she thought.

As they approached the farm, she could see Thumblerock and a few animals loading a cart in the yard. It was being filled with sacks and barrels. A large donkey was gripping a particularly heavy sack between its teeth whilst lifting it onto the back of the cart.

Thumblerock was waving his arms and pointing here and there as other animals scurried around following his directions. He turned and saw them approaching, and then waved before running off into the barn, narrowly missing the revolving sails from the windmill.

Alannah spoke to the horses, and their cart glided up to the entrance of the farmhouse. She jumped down and helped Rosie.

"If you would like to go and change from those riding clothes and freshen up? Don't be long; Rocky will get impatient," she said, grinning.

They both went into the kitchen where Rosie took off her boots and ran upstairs. When she came back down wearing her freshly laundered jeans, shirt and jacket, Alannah unclipped Rosie's motivator from the box on the wall and handed it to her.

"You may need this to help with translation if we get separated. I've assumed you will want to have a look around by yourself. I have a few errands to run and some stores to pick up."

"Oh, okay," said Rosie. She slipped the little glowing box into a top pocket of her coat and zipped it up.

Chapter 5 Courage

The cart in the farmyard was now full with produce for the market. Thumblerock was the last to jump up into his seat.

Rosie suddenly shouted, "Hattie! Hattie! I haven't seen her. Will she be joining us?"

"Oh, I should have mentioned," said Thumblerock. "We can't take Hattie to the market – the experience and the noise would overwhelm her. She's still developing her language skills with the other animals. I think all the life on the farm is sufficient for her to come to terms with for now."

At that moment, Hattie emerged from behind one of the stable doors. She'd obviously been snoozing as straw was stuck in her fur. She stretched out her full body as dogs do after a nap. She looked up at Rosie and barked.

"Can I just say hello before we go? It seems an age since I've seen her."

"Of course," said Alannah.

Rosie jumped out of the cart and ran over to her. "Hi, Hattie, how are you doing?" Rosie rubbed her head and neck.

Hattie murmured, then stuck her head between Rosie's arm and body as though she were hiding. Rosie recognised it as a sign of affection.

"I'm sorry, but you can't come with us this afternoon. We won't be long, though." Which is what all dog owners say to their pets when they are going out!

This time Hattie didn't look at all miserable. She barked, then a quick spin and took off back to the stable. Rosie laughed and climbed back into the cart.

"She's obviously having a ball," said Rosie.

"You've said that before," said Alannah. "What does it mean?"

"I guess it's just having a great time – enjoying herself."

"Oh, I see," said Alannah, looking none the wiser.

Thumblerock placed his motivator into a box with a satisfying click and spoke softly. The cart began to roll gently out of the yard.

Before Rosie could ask the question, Alannah answered, "We will always use a motivator when we have a heavy load to transport. It's unnecessary and unfair to ask any of the horses to pull it. They have enough to do on the farm."

"I understand," said Rosie. "It makes perfect sense. How far is the market?"

"It's about a half hour's ride," said Thumblerock. "The road will get busy as we approach the village."

They left the farm track and turned onto the lane, the same lane they had arrived on the day before. This time they turned the opposite way. The cart picked up speed as it ran along the smooth road surface.

On each side of the road, farm tracks peeled off towards other dwellings. Rosie reckoned they were travelling at about forty miles an hour. The difference from being at home was the quiet and effortless progress. Uphill and down dale, they swept towards the village. Rosie noticed signs pointing here and there with a language she couldn't decipher.

"What's the village called?"

"Harlsey," said Alannah.

"That sounds like a village near to where I live."

"You will notice lots of similarities," said Alannah. "It's not because they are similar, it's just the way the motivator is translating the words from our language into yours."

"It's fascinating how the technology works," said Rosie. She then thought of another interesting and fundamental question to ask. "Before the motivators, could you speak with all the animals?"

Thumblerock and Alannah both turned to look at Rosie, quite astonished by her question.

"No, no, Rosie, we couldn't," replied Thumblerock. "Our existence before the discovery of the motivator crystal was, I'm sure, similar to your world."

"How long ago was that?" asked Rosie.

"Well, it was about a thousand cycles ago. It's a day when we celebrate each cycle. By a cycle, I mean a year. It's the biggest festival we have."

"You're a smart girl, Rosie," said Alannah. "Your great-grandfather never asked us a question like that."

Thumblerock added, "The upheaval it caused on our world took many generations to sort out. The balance you see now has taken a lot of effort on everyone's part to achieve."

"I wonder if we have the crystal on our world?" asked Rosie.

"You have," said Thumblerock. "Otherwise, your world would not be part of the network. Your planet, as with many others, is linked across the expanse of our galaxy. It's the crystal embedded in the planets mantle that invisibly links all of us. Like a spider's web stretching out across the stars."

"Why haven't you shown us how to find it and use it?" asked Rosie.

"That's a good question. The Council after many centuries of debate decided not to interfere in the development of other worlds. The turmoil and upheaval it caused here could be repeated elsewhere with dire consequences. They didn't want to be blamed or have to take any responsibility. Each world should be allowed to develop in its own way, with or without the discovery of the motivator crystal," replied Thumblerock. "This is why we only make individual contact with civilised worlds like your own. As you know, this is limited to every three generations. From this, we can monitor how each society is developing and whether contact should be broadened. If we believe a society is ready."

"Is our world ready?" asked Rosie.

"Well, that's not a question I can answer. Perhaps it's a question for the Council when you meet with them."

"How do you assess the readiness of a planet through its children?"

"Another good question, which I can try and answer for you," he said. "Your motivator, if I can explain simply, is connected to your mind – your brainwaves, in simpler terms. It monitors all your reactions and responses to everyday activities, such as conflicts, relationships, decision making, for example. These attributes are graded against a series of markers. We only need a few days to collect the intelligence required to make informed decisions."

"Why children?" asked Rosie.

"Well, we see you as young adults. Old enough to understand and react to situations instinctively and honestly. An adult can react in different ways through learned behaviours. This does not give us the profile information we need. Does that make any sense?"

"Yes, I think so."

Rosie passed the remainder of the journey thinking about Thumblerock's explanation and soaking up the views and the differences she could identify between the Earth and Damianos. They were more similar than different. Green grass, trees, bushes, flowers, rivers, horses and all the other animals. A few indistinct creatures she didn't recognise; otherwise, it was like the Earth, only on steroids. Even the clouds drifted enormously through the big blue of the heavens.

A little while later, a few other roads came into view converging with their own onto a broad, paved thoroughfare. Carriages and carts filtered in seamlessly, obviously controlled by the motivators. Trolls of all different shapes and sizes waved and shouted greetings.

Suddenly, she saw children, young Trolls accompanying their parents. This was the first time she'd seen youngsters. It was a question she'd been tempted to ask Alannah but hadn't found the right moment. Perhaps it was a question for later once they had returned from the market.

The village then came into view. Single-storey buildings for the most part on the outskirts progressively raising up to two and three stories as they travelled further into the community. The cart came to rest outside a large warehouse with an opening on the first floor above them. A platform descended to the floor and arrived with a solid clunk. A Troll was holding onto a rail above them and leaning out whilst shouting down to Thumblerock.

"Rosie," said Alannah. "We'll leave Rocky to unload the cart, and he'll meet us in the market once he's finished his business."

"Okay," she replied before jumping down behind Alannah, with a little help. They waved to Rocky, and off they went through a passageway towards the noisy market.

They emerged into a large broad tree-lined street. Market stalls were positioned on each side underneath the overhanging tree canopy. There was an amazing display of bright and colourful goods. Food, clothing, flowers, pots and pans, tools, toys, art, and other odd objects she didn't recognise. Somewhere in the background, she could hear some beautiful melodic music.

She was overwhelmed – not only amazed at the scene, but she was also so small amongst the melee of huge Trolls surrounding her. Alannah held her hand as she navigated a pass through to a more open area. She was also attracting attention with both adult and young Trolls staring at her and waving. She waved back, feeling a little like a celebrity.

"Let's go and have a cool drink at the café over there," said Alannah. "From there you can see a good part of the whole market." She was pointing to a terrace with some steps up to it. Some Trolls were sitting watching the world go by as they took refreshments.

Alannah led Rosie up some stairs and found a free table. It was a round wooden pedestal table with mushroom-shaped stools firmly fixed around it. Above it, a substantial thatched umbrella shielded the table from both the weather and the bright starlight. Rosie was helped to climb onto a stool and sat, with her legs swinging at least a metre from the floor. Alannah took a seat opposite and smiled at Rosie, who was grinning wildly at the scene below.

A young male Troll was walking down the middle of the street playing a flute or something similar. That was the music she'd heard. He was dressed in a colourful tunic, all the rainbow colours of the motivator crystal. Behind him, children in similar outfits danced and sang to the tune. Coins were tossed into a hat held by one of the youngsters from appreciative onlookers.

"You have money, then?" asked Rosie to Alannah.

"Yes of course," she replied. "It forms a small part of our economy. For the most part, we use a bartering system. No one is encouraged to hold large quantities of coin, just enough to trade for items we can't barter with. With the discovery of the motivator crystal, there was no need to hoard wealth. We have all the power we need to live comfortably. An individual can choose how to serve the community they live in, by farming in our case. Also making things or providing services, like this refreshment shop."

"What if someone wants to hoard money or break the rules in some other way?"

"There are always some individuals who don't want to live under our system," said Alannah, "as there will be on your world."

"Yes," said Rosie. "We have prisons for them. If they break the law, we lock them up."

Alannah nodded. "If we can't rehabilitate individuals, they have the option to leave our society. There are many other worlds we are connected to. They can go and pursue an individual way of life. We rarely have to imprison any Troll. For the most part, we are a peaceful society; at least we are now that we have balance."

A tall blonde female Troll and a youngster approached their table and smiled at Alannah and Rosie. Alannah stood up and embraced her politely.

"Rosie, this is Titania. She is a close friend and neighbour of ours, and this is her son Callisto."

Rosie attempted to jump off her chair, but thought better of it as she would look silly being so small in their company. Instead, she held out her hand in greeting. Titania and Callisto both laughed at the gesture but gracefully accepted her hand in turn.

"Would you like to join us?" asked Alannah.

"We would be honoured to sit with you and Rosie for a while," said Titania. "Alannah told us you were visiting from Earth. How do the riding dungarees fit?"

"Oh," said Rosie, "perfectly thank you. They were your daughter's? Alannah told me."

"Yes, when she was a young child," said Titania.

"I must seem so small to you," said Rosie. "I'm sorry."

"Please don't apologise. I meant no disrespect; you are a most welcome and an honoured guest in our community."

The two female Trolls then began a conversation, so Rosie turned to Callisto and asked, "How old are you?"

"I'm twelve cycles," replied Callisto.

"Not sure what that means exactly. Thumblerock mentioned it before?" said Rosie.

"To us it means one circuit of our star equals a cycle," he said.

"Same as on Earth, then," said Rosie. "I'm twelve cycles, too."

"If they allow us," said Callisto excitedly, "would you like to see the river and the fish slide? It's more fun than the boring old market?"

Before she could answer, Callisto was pleading with his mother and Alannah to let them go. Rosie was a little peeved as she was looking forward to seeing some of the stalls.

"I don't mind going with him," said Rosie. "As long as you can show me around the market before we leave?" she said to Alannah.

Alannah looked at her and said, "Please be careful, and don't let him talk you into doing anything you don't want to do."

"Yes," said Titania to her son. "I expect Rosie is the sensible one here. As soon as she wants to come back, we will be in the market, so don't be long. Hold her hand so she doesn't get lost."

Callisto helped Rosie off her seat, and she followed him as quickly as she could down the stairs. She purposefully gripped his hand as they set off across the market street.

The Trolls in the market were all respectful and made space when they saw Rosie being dragged along behind Callisto.

One shouted at him. "Slow down, boy. You'll run her little legs off."

"I'm sorry, Rosie. I'll slow down for you."

"Might be slow for you," said Rosie. "I can't keep up with this pace. Is there a fire? What's the rush?"

Callisto stopped and looked at her a bit bemused as he considered her words, then grinned. "That's funny," he said. "Now I understand your meaning. Do all humans from Earth make tragic jokes?"

"Yes," said Rosie. "All the time."

It worked: Callisto slowed to a gentle stroll, which was still quite quick but a lot more comfortable.

They ducked behind a market stall and headed down some wide steps towards a broad river. This curled away in the distance to what she assumed was the sea. Even here there were market stalls strung out along the riverside with huge baskets of fish, ropes, nets and all sorts of general fishing tackle. Behind the stalls, large fishing boats and other craft were moored up against the dock with lots of activity to and fro between the boats and the dockside.

"Over there," said Callisto, pointing. "The fish slide – it's brilliant to watch."

A large boat was being unloaded by a crane with a huge bucket. It was completely silent except for the clanking of metal. Rosie was still surprised at the quietness of this industrial scene. She couldn't hear any engines whining or see diesel smoke belching out of exhausts. The bucket swung around, then opened its jaws, spewing fish onto a wide metal channel which ran down into a warehouse below the dock.

Large silvery fish slithered and slapped their way down the slide. Callisto sat on his haunches and pointed out all the various types of fish whizzing past. He was wide-eyed and excited. Rosie was a little unimpressed; the process didn't really keep her attention.

"I want to be a fishing Troll when I'm an adult," he said. "Do you have fishing boats on Earth?"

"We do," said Rosie. "A lot of people depend on it for their livelihood."

"A fishing Troll only works for half a cycle each year," said Callisto. "That would suit me just fine."

"Is that so you don't take too many fish from the sea?" asked Rosie.

"I think so," said Callisto. "I'd also get half a cycle off without having to work."

The next moment, Callisto, leaning too far over, suddenly lost his footing and fell headlong at least two metres down onto the fish slide with a heavy bump. He screamed out in pain and fought frantically, trying to keep hold of the sides of the slide to stop himself being washed away. A mixture of fish and sea water swirled past him, trying to drag him down towards the warehouse.

Rosie frantically looked around. No one had seen the accident. What should she do? Everyone else was too far away to help.

"Hold on!" she shouted to a panicking Callisto. She looked behind her and spotted a coil of rope wrapped around a mooring pin. She ran across and grabbed it. It was heavy, so she dragged it with both hands laboriously back to the edge of the slide. The rope was almost as thick as her whole hand, so she struggled to work with it. She wrapped one of the ends around a nearby lamp post, then created a double loop slip knot. She knew any weight pulling on the other end would tighten the knot to the post, so it would not give way.

Looking over the edge of the slide, Callisto was still there desperately gripping onto the rim of the slide and screaming at her for help. By this time, he'd attracted some attention. Trolls were running towards them, but they were still some distance away.

Rosie started to feed the heavy rope down towards Callisto. He looked up as she yelled at him, "When the rope reaches you, try and wrap a few coils around your left wrist and arm, then let go of the side. I've tied it to a post, so it will hold your weight."

Callisto, wild-eyed and frightened, managed to nod at her as he watched the rope advancing towards him.

Fish and freezing sea water were slapping him painfully around the head as he took one hand from the edge of the slide and grabbed the approaching rope. As Rosie suggested, he curled the rope around his wrist and arm a few times, and then took a strong grip. He let go of the slide and gripped the rope with the other hand. Immediately, he swung out into the centre of the slide and dropped down a further few metres until the rope suddenly stretched out and tightened around the lamp post. He winced with pain as the rope bit into his arm, but he was secure for the moment.

Help had now arrived. A male Troll with curly black hair tied up in a ponytail looked over the side of the fish slide and quickly assessed the situation.

He turned to Rosie, patted her shoulder and said, "Good work." He looked at the taut line and the knot tied to the post, and then grabbed the rope to abseil down towards Callisto. He proceeded past him and tied the trailing rope around his middle. Kneeling up at an angle to the slope, he moved himself forward taking Callisto's weight. By grabbing the rope in front of him, it began to slacken the grip on his arm. With the young Troll now firmly in his grasp, he waited for more assistance to haul them both out of the slide.

Several other dock workers were now on the scene, and the two of them were quickly brought out. Callisto was in real pain from the fall and the damage to his arm. Tears were running down his cheeks and he was clearly in shock. Rosie took a step back as quite a crowd had now built up and she didn't want to get trampled.

"That's Titania's boy," she heard a voice shout. "I've just seen her in the market."

"Well, run and fetch her quickly and find the healer." A few Trolls ran off in different directions following the instructions.

The Troll who had rescued Callisto pushed through the crowd and headed towards Rosie, who was now sitting on the side of the jetty.

"Real quick thinking for such a small person," he said to Rosie. "I reckon you saved his life. If he'd gone down into the warehouse bins, he would have been covered in tons of fish."

Rosie looked up at him with tears running down her cheeks. She was clearly in shock as well.

He sat down next to her. "My name is Aldebaran. What's yours?"

"I'm Rosie," she sobbed. "Will he be all right?"

"He'll be just fine. He has some cuts and bruises to his arm and a large bump on the head, but Trolls have thick skulls." Rosie smiled a little.

They both sat quietly together on the dockside for a few minutes, Aldebaran put his arm around Rosie to comfort her. She was shivering and feeling a little sick. Across the dock, she could see some Trolls running with a stretcher towards Callisto. They were closely followed by a medical Troll, and Titania and Alannah, who both looked horrified.

Rosie raised her hand weakly and waved at them. Alannah saw her first and shouted to Titania, sending her to her son.

Alannah composed herself a little as she hurried over to Rosie. She sat down on Rosie's other side and cuddled her. Rosie couldn't speak, so Aldebaran explained what had happened as far as he knew.

A few moments later, Titania came running over to where they were all sat and knelt in front of them.

Rosie looked at her concerned face. "Is he all right?"

"He is. A little bumped, bruised and embarrassed, otherwise he's fine. Your quick thinking saved his life. You've acted so heroically; I don't know how our family and community could ever repay you. Our children are so valuable to us."

Looking up at Titania, Rosie said, "I'm just happy he's okay. Please don't feel indebted to me. I'm sure he would have done the same for me if our roles had been reversed."

"I have a feeling," said Titania, "that you wouldn't have put yourself in that situation."

Rosie smiled and said, "Probably not, but boys will be boys." All of them burst out laughing.

"Exactly," said Titania. "A perfect expression." She turned to Aldebaran. "Can I also thank you for coming to their rescue. We are all so grateful."

"I'm happy to be of service, ma'am, and very impressed with the knot the little lady tied. A professional job; she'd be welcome on my boat anytime."

"I must go with him now, Rosie. They are taking him to the medical facility to be thoroughly checked over. I'd love you to pay us a visit tomorrow so we can thank you properly?"

"I'd like that," said Rosie.

Titania stood up and returned to the side of her son, who was now being carried towards the steps to the village followed by the medical Troll.

"Are you feeling up to returning to the market, Rosie?" said Alannah. "Rocky will be wondering where we've got to."

"Yes, perhaps a little shopping therapy would do the trick," said Rosie.

Both Alannah and Aldebaran burst into howls of laughter. Some bystanders looked at them a little confused.

"I love the human way of coping with trauma," said Alannah. "Your grandfather always had us in stitches laughing. You're such an evocative species. It's such a shame..." Alannah cut her sentence short, as if she'd spoken out of turn.

Rosie considered her words but just smiled. "I'm ready. Let's go."

"Thank you, Aldebaran. Thank you for being there and helping both of them." Alannah hugged him politely.

"Glad I could be of service. Goodbye, Rosie, hope we meet again." Aldebaran turned and strode away to his colleagues who were patting him on the back as Rosie and Alannah left the dockside.

A crowd of Trolls were on the stairs, and they parted to each side as Rosie and Alannah climbed up towards the market. News had obviously travelled fast about the accident and the little girl from Earth. All at once, they started clapping as she climbed the steps. It was now time for Rosie to feel embarrassed. She tried to cover up her blushes by smiling and nodding.

"Well, you've become quite a celebrity in our community, Rosie," said Alannah, "and well deserved."

"Oh, please, can we stop talking about it. It makes making me feel so uncomfortable." As they reached the market, normal activity took over. Rosie was relieved.

They found Thumblerock soon after. Unfortunately for Rosie, he hadn't heard the news. As soon as Alannah started telling him, he picked up Rosie and hugged her tightly.

"Come on," he said. "I need a cold drink, and you can tell me all about it."

They returned to the café. Rosie allowed Alannah to tell the whole story again as Thumblerock grinned at Rosie.

"He's a menace that child," said Thumblerock. "Could have killed them both. What if he'd dragged her in too?"

"Well, that didn't happen, Rocky, so no need to speculate," said Alannah. "It's just a good job Rosie was there to save the day. You can talk," she added. "The scrapes you got into as a youngster."

"Who taught you about knots?" asked Thumblerock.

"Scouts," said Rosie. Thumblerock looked confused. "It's an activity group for girls and boys outside of school. It teaches us all sorts of fun things like camping, canoeing or climbing, and lots of charitable activities for the communities we live in. That's where I learnt about knots."

"Well, well done, Rosie, I'm proud of you."

They all sat on the terrace for a little while watching the activity in the market. A young male Troll brought them some cordial in a jug with lots of ice and a selection of fruits floating on top. It was delicious. Rosie drank two full glasses before she was satisfied. The whole ordeal had left her thirsty and exhausted.

They walked slowly back through the market, Alannah stopping here and there to show Rosie some of the more interesting stalls and small shops. An old Troll bent in the back hobbled out of one, leant down to Rosie and handed her a beautifully carved and painted horse and cart. It was small and intricate, with leather straps and brass fixings. Thumblerock moved towards him to offer some coins. The old Troll held up his hand in refusal, lay his palm on Rosie's head, turned, and then went back into his shop without a word.

They walked on out of the market and through the alleyway, back to where Thumblerock had left the cart.

"This is so beautiful," said Rosie, studying the model. "I'll treasure it always."

They loaded up what stores they'd acquired from the market and sat back on the leather bench seat. Thumblerock attached his motivator, spoke some words and the cart glided swiftly out of its parking space and headed up the lane out of the village.

Alannah and Thumblerock chatted casually as they progressed towards the farm. Rosie had fallen asleep between them and gripping her new gift. There was little to say about the journey home. It had been an eventful day with quite enough excitement for all of them.

As they turned onto the lane for the farm, Hattie was sat waiting with another dog. A large black and white sheep dog. They both started barking as the cart came into view, which woke Rosie.

"Do you mind if I walk the rest of the way with the dogs? I need to stretch my legs. What's the other dog's name?"

"He's called Taurus," said Thumblerock. "Of course, take your time."

Rosie jumped down from the cart, and the two dogs greeted her as though she'd been away for weeks. The cart rolled away as she wandered slowly down the lane towards the farm. Both dogs rummaged here and there sniffing with undefined excitement. It was a beautiful evening, no breeze at all, with soft warm starlight, and melodic birdsong drifting in from all directions.

She watched the dogs as she walked. She presumed they were calling each other every few seconds.

"Look over here – that's a great smell."

"No, over here, it's much better."

"Well, what is it?"

"I don't know – have a sniff yourself."

"Okay, I'm coming."

She watched them all the way back to the farm and realised that even though Hattie was now talking with her new friends, her life was still simple. She felt a little jealous. In a day or so, she was due to meet the Council. Rosie assumed her own life was about to become more complicated in ways she couldn't imagine.

Chapter 6 Going Solo

She woke up the next morning, sprang out of bed and put on the riding dungarees that were hanging over her chair. When she arrived in the kitchen, both Thumblerock and Alannah were sat at the table having breakfast.

"Morning, Rosie," they both said. "How are you today?"

"I'm good thanks," she replied. "It looks like another beautiful day."

"It is," said Thumblerock, "although we may get a rain shower later. Do you still want to go out with Quizzical?"

"Oh yes, I'm really looking forward to it. Can Hattie come with me? I've hardly seen her these past few days."

"Of course," said Thumblerock. "She said the same to me last evening."

"I've spoken with Quizzical," said Alannah. "I've asked her to take you later in the day to the farm where Callisto and his family live. They are eager you should drop by to see them after yesterday's calamity."

Rosie nodded a little anxiously.

"Don't worry. Titania understands that you don't want a fuss. They just want to say thank you. They've invited us all for dinner, so you won't be on your own."

"Okay, I'd like to see him again," said Rosie.

"Oh, and Rosie, you need to take your motivator today so the animals can understand you."

"Do you have any children?" asked Rosie, quite out of the blue. "It's just I've been wondering these past few days – there doesn't seem to be a lot of children around."

Thumblerock sighed. "No, we don't," he said. "It's a little more complicated than you might imagine. It's not that we didn't want them, it's just society decided many generations ago that we needed to control our population and its impact on the planet. Decisions were made, and it was agreed that keeping our world in balance was the main priority. Especially with the discovery of the motivator crystal. With almost limitless free power, the whole basis of our future society needed careful consideration." Thumblerock continued, "Each couple must apply to be parents, and there are lots of reasons which can exclude couples. For us, my role with the Council and travelling off-world excluded us immediately. We knew that and accepted it; it can be a dangerous occupation. Does that make any sense to you, Rosie?"

"Yes, I think so," she said.

"Don't think it's a hardship for us, though. We are so lucky, and get to meet wonderful people like yourself and your great-grandfather from all around our galaxy. We also have the farm where we live together with all the other animals and help them as much as we can."

"I understand," she said. "I love it here; it's just so peaceful." She glanced at Alannah, who turned away and left the table. She seemed a little upset by the conversation.

After breakfast, Alannah took Rosie and Hattie to the barn to meet again with Quizzical. "I've packed some snacks in your bag, and Quizzical knows where to go. She's also under strict instructions to keep out of trouble. I have a feeling I shouldn't worry too much; your great-grandfather, however, was a completely different story. He didn't know, but we even sent some birds to follow him when he was out alone or with Quizzical."

Rosie laughed. "Oh, please don't worry. I just want a quiet day. I'll meet you all later."

Quizzical was stood with Hattie waiting for them. She bowed to Rosie and Alannah who returned the gesture. Alannah lifted Rosie onto the horse's broad back and spoke to the horse quietly with her hand placed on the side of her beautiful face. The horse whinnied and nodded, then slowly walked out of the barn with Hattie following. Rosie turned and waved as they left the farmyard.

The horse trotted along the track towards the main road and turned right at the junction in the direction of the village. Two or three carriages sailed silently past as they walked along the side of the road. The occupants smiled, clapped and waved madly at her as they went by. Obviously, the news of the previous day had spread far and wide. Rosie felt a little uncomfortable about this adulation. She was pleased when Quizzical veered off the road onto a leafy lane.

It was obviously an ancient trail; she was aware of this as its level dropped down well below the fields on either side. From her lofty position on the horse, she could just about see through the bottom of the hedges on each side of the path. She remembered this geographical feature from lessons at school. Ancient paths developed into these deep culverts between pastureland over many centuries of use.

As the horse continued along the path, the hedges became even more established, which blocked the light from the star overhead. It created a chilled, quiet atmosphere. Rosie could only hear the horse breathing, its softened footsteps and Hattie grumbling below her.

"Don't worry, guys," she said. "I'm sure it won't last long." She said this for her own benefit as well; it was making her feel a little nervous, too.

After a few more minutes, they emerged into the bright daylight at the top of a slope. A lonely old wooden gate, at least three metres high, barred their way across the track.

The horse wandered slowly to one side of the gate and bit into a rope looped over the gate post. She lifted it over the top and let go, freeing the gate to slowly swing open. Once they'd passed through, she turned and pushed the gate closed with her nose and put the rope loop back over the post.

"Clever girl. I would never have been able to reach it."

Looking at her from the corner of its eye, Quizzical shook her head. Rosie assumed she was saying you're welcome.

Below them, the valley opened out like a bowl. A river wound its way through and spilt into a long, broad lake. There was a sandy shore on the nearside, and it was heavily forested on the other.

Quizzical continued down the path towards it. Hattie was running ahead sniffing the vegetation and chewing the odd bit of grass. Just before they reached the edge of the lake, the horse stopped next to a high fence. She turned her head and nudged Rosie's leg. At first, Rosie didn't quite understand, so Hattie ran around in a circle and barked.

"Oh, you want me to get off and use the fence to climb down?" she said aloud.

Hattie raised her head and barked once, and the horse nodded.

"This is a lovely place for a picnic," said Rosie. "A good choice." She carefully placed her hand on the fence and then her foot and swung her other leg over the horse. Once she had a tight hold on the fence, Quizzical moved away to let her climb down. Rosie realised that she was quite stiff. She wasn't used to horse riding; her legs and back were aching.

Back on the ground, she greeted Hattie with a head rub, then wandered over to the lake shore and sat down. Hattie and Quizzical seemed to be in conversation; they both looked at her as if asking a question. As she didn't respond, they both thought for a moment before suddenly charging into the water. Rosie howled with laughter.

"That's what you wanted, to go for a swim. Well, it's a warm day – I don't blame you."

Both animals were good swimmers. In fact, Rosie knew it was probably Hattie's favourite thing to do. Off she went straight out into the lake with her tail rotating behind her like a propeller. Quizzical was not far behind, snorting and calling. She watched them playing for about ten minutes until they came out, and then shook water droplets all over her.

"Thanks, guys."

Rosie then opened her backpack to see what was inside. Some sandwiches wrapped in paper, something that looked like a sausage roll, some cake and a bottle of fruit juice. Also, there were some large carrots and dog biscuits. Alannah had thought of everything. She gave the snacks to the animals, and they both wandered off to crunch and chew at their leisure. Quizzical then started to crop some grass, and Hattie returned to Rosie's side to stretch out for a snooze.

All along the water's edge as far as she could see, birds were busy. Some waders, ducks and some smaller birds darting in and out taking a bath in the shallow water's edge. After a while, Rosie and Hattie got up and wandered along the shore. She shouted to Quizzical, telling her what they were doing. The horse whinnied and continued eating grass.

It must have been early afternoon. She had promised Alannah they would head for the farm where Callisto lived well before the sun went down. She took off her boots and walked along the sand by the water's edge with Hattie. It was beautifully still and tranquil. After about ten minutes meandering, she suddenly stopped. Something wasn't quite right.

Just in front of her were at least three sets of boot prints clearly defined in the damp sand. Two sets were obviously Trolls by their sheer size and the square front of the boot. The third set, however, looked just like a human's hiking boot. The sole pattern was clearly displayed in the sand. An adult human, in fact, as they were much bigger prints than Rosie's boots were making. She was stunned. Rocky had told her that she was the only visitor from Earth on Damianos. Was that true?

For good measure, Rosie placed her boot next to this print to compare the contours against her own. There was no doubt. They were human, and she could see part of a brand name, at least a few letters. She nervously scanned the horizon up and down the lake shore. Perhaps they were still here. She calmed herself a little. It didn't seem as though anyone was around. *Let's just see where they go,* she thought.

"Hattie," she said. "If you understand me, can we follow these prints in the sand for a while?"

She sniffed at the prints, looked up at her, barked and headed back towards Quizzical, who was at least eight hundred metres away.

"Okay," said Rosie. "I understand. Good idea – let's go and get Quizzical first." Rosie ran after Hattie. She didn't realise just how far she'd gone, and was quite out of breath by the time she reached the horse.

Rosie told Quizzical that she wanted to follow some footprints she'd found on the beach. Quizzical nodded her head up and down, and then walked back to the fence a little way back up the track. Rosie followed her, climbed the fence and onto the horse's back. They set off at a canter along the lake shore and arrived at the first sign of the footprints in just a few minutes.

"I don't want to walk over the prints and spoil them, so let's just move a metre to one side and follow them for a while." They walked along the beach next to the water with the prints on the upper side of the beach. All three sets were quite close together, so they were obviously made at the same time, as if the three individuals were walking together. The only other prints on the beach were animals and birds.

They followed the prints for about half an hour. After turning a corner, a small inlet opened out in front of them with an old wooden jetty extending out into the deeper water. The prints ended at the jetty. Rosie scoured the lakeside ahead and across to the other side. She could see a small boat tied up to a similar jetty on the opposite side of the lake, just in front of the treeline. She guessed it was probably about a kilometre across the water. There didn't seem to be any activity on the far shore, although she could see a path leading away through the trees.

At that moment, it began to rain. Just a light shower, although Rosie could see some ominous dark clouds approaching from behind her. Quizzical whinnied again and began to turn around.

"You're right, Quizzical," she said. "We can't follow any further. Let's set off for Callisto's farm. I think we are going to get a bit wet, Hattie."

Hattie barked and looked a bit sullen as raindrops started to splash off her head and nose.

Rosie pulled her coat out of her bag, put it on and zipped it up as far as she could. Quizzical set off at a good pace, and Rosie clung onto the ring on the front of the saddle. She was enjoying the rush of wind and rain against her face. Hattie ran alongside. She didn't look troubled with the pace; however, Rosie was thinking that she'd be stiff tonight. Quizzical was probably having the same thoughts and slowed a little.

They went past the end of the track where they had picnicked and followed the lake along the shore for another kilometre or so. Another track peeled off up through the fields, and she could see a farm in the distance a fair way off through the rain.

By the time they clopped into the farmyard, all three of them were soaked to the skin and looking miserable. Quizzical walked straight into the barn out of the rain. Hattie ran in and rolled on the first patch of straw she could find, making happy grunting noises. A tall young female Troll was at the far end of the barn raking straw. She looked up with surprise, and then smiled before throwing down her folk and coming over to greet them.

"Hello," she said to Rosie. She also said something to Quizzical and Hattie, which Rosie didn't catch. "I'm Celaeno, Callisto's older sister. You must be Rosie; I've heard so much about you. Here, let me help you from Quizzical." Celaeno was tall and slim with blonde almost white hair. She effortlessly lifted Rosie down from the horse.

Once standing, Rosie looked up at her. She was tall, about 1.8 metres she estimated, with curly blonde hair, a broad pleasant face and a lovely smile.

"Come on, let's get into the house and get you out of those wet clothes. The others are not home yet, so we can have a chat by the fire. I'm really keen to hear all about your world." Celaeno removed the saddle from Quizzical and left her in a stall with plenty of fresh straw.

Rosie, Hattie and Celaeno left the barn and ran quickly across the yard towards the house. They entered a large boot room with stone flags and whitewashed walls.

Celaeno took Rosie's coat and boots and hung them on some pegs above a large boiler, which glowed colourfully through the glass. "Follow me," she said.

They walked through into a large kitchen with wooden units all around, and a beautifully carved oak table with chairs and a lovely glowing fire in the corner.

"Take your clothes off by the fire, and I'll go and find you something to wear."

Rosie quickly stripped off any wet layers and rubbed her long hair with a towel Celaeno had given her. Celaeno returned with some maroon moleskin dungarees and a white blouse. Rosie pulled them on. They were a little big, but she didn't mind as she was now warm and comfortable.

"I'll soon have these dry for you," said Celaeno. She went back into the boot room with the wet clothes.

"What time do you expect them back?" asked Rosie. "I've seen something very surprising on the beach – I really need to tell Rocky."

"Oh, not long. They've taken Callisto to the local medical centre for a check over. Tell me, Rosie, what's troubled you?"

She told her about the footprints on the beach. Celaeno was also shocked and concerned.

"I've never heard of such a thing," she said. "All I know is travel between the outlying worlds such as Earth is tightly restricted. Only Thumblerock has permission to travel there from this world, and only he would bring visitors back like yourself."

Rosie started to cry. "The problem is that they may not believe me. I've been worrying about it on my way through the rain. It will no doubt clear any footprints from the beach."

"Rosie," said Celaeno, comforting her, "don't forget, both Quizzical and Hattie have also seen and followed the prints, so you have two other reliable witnesses to your story."

"Of course, how silly of me," she said, feeling a little better.

"They'll be back soon," said Celaeno. "You can tell your story. Thumblerock will know what to do. It is peculiar, though. Anyway, cheer up. Let the adults worry about such things." She then added, "You're quite a celebrity in our community, and you've only been here a few days."

Rosie smiled. She liked Celaeno: she was uncomplicated and direct. "Please don't think of me as a hero. I was just in the right place at the right time."

"Aargh, my brother," said Celaeno. "If anyone were going to fall into the fish slide, it would be him. You wouldn't believe the scrapes he's got into. It's a good job you were there to save the day. We are all so grateful. He can be a pain, but I wouldn't want to be without him. Thank you, Rosie."

"Can we change the subject?" asked Rosie. "You wanted to know about my world. What can I tell you?"

"Your family, tell me about them?"

"Well, I have a younger sister who is ten years old called Mollie, my mum, dad and Kato our pet cat. We live in a house in a market town, not unlike Harlsey. The main difference between our worlds is that ours is very busy with billions of people cars, lorries, planes, and everyone is in a hurry."

"What are cars, lorries and planes?" asked Celaeno.

"They are modes of transport. The car is like your carriages, and lorries are much bigger and move stuff around, like food for instance. Planes fly in the sky, so we can travel quickly around the planet. Here it seems so much quieter, or is this an underpopulated area?"

"No, I wouldn't say so," replied Celaeno. "Obviously, towns and villages have more people, but we are living out in the countryside. You're going to Sculptor the Central Domain soon I believe?" asked Celaeno. "You will find it much busier with lots of people and activity. I've been a few times – it's amazing. Lots of shops and things to do, as well as boys." Rosie laughed. "Callisto and I love to go. It's such a treat. It can get boring on the farm."

"You must have friends around here?" said Rosie.

"Yes, of course. A few close by and more from school in the village."

"I wonder if you could come with us to Sculptor?" said Rosie. "I'd like that, having someone more my age to talk to. It's a bit awkward sometimes with just Thumblerock and Alannah. They are so kind and lovely to me; however, my reason for being here does seem to weigh heavy on them. I can sense it."

"I'd love that, too," said Celaeno. "It's been over a cycle since I've been. I could take you shopping and there are the young adult activity centres to show you, where we can meet boys." Rosie laughed again.

"I don't expect they'll be interested in me," she said.

"Oh, you'd be the star of the show – no doubt." They both laughed together.

Two carts rolled into the yard. Rosie could see Thumblerock jumping down from one. He saw her through the window and waved. There was a lot of commotion, then the kitchen door burst open and Titania rushed in. She immediately ran to Rosie, picked her up like a rag doll and cuddled her.

"How's our little hero?" she said.

"Mum," said Celaeno, "she doesn't want a fuss. You're embarrassing her."

"Oh yes, I'm sorry," she said before carefully putting her down.

"I'm fine," said Rosie. "How's Callisto?"

"He's on the mend," she said. "Not much harm done, thank goodness."

The rest of the party were now all in the kitchen. Thumblerock and Alannah stood back as Callisto and another male Troll, obviously his father, approached Rosie.

Callisto said, "Hello, Rosie, I'm pleased to see you again."

"Me too. How are you feeling?"

"Oh, I'm fine. A little achy; it's nothing really." Rosie could tell that he was still in some pain. His arm was bandaged in a sling and the side of his face was badly bruised.

"I'm so pleased you're feeling better," she said.

Callisto beamed at her. "I apologise for causing all this trouble."

"You're a boy," said Rosie. "Just as on my world, always getting into scrapes. Think nothing of it." She laughed, and Callisto and Celaeno laughed, too. Then they all started laughing, which broke the ice perfectly.

The other male Troll then approached Rosie and knelt down taking her hand in his. "I'm Atlas, Callisto's father. I know you don't want a fuss, Rosie, so all I will say is thank you on behalf of us all. You performed a service for us, which we may never be able to repay. We would like you to accept a small token of our esteem."

Titania handed her husband a small black leather case. He opened it and presented it to Rosie.

She took the small box with one hand and gasped as she looked at the jewel inside. It was an eight-pointed star with crystallised arms radiating outwards. In the centre was a fluorescent steely blue gem.

"Lift it out," he said.

Rosie carefully lifted the star from the box and lay it across the palm of her hand.

"Do you have your motivator?" asked Atlas. "Touch it to the centre of the jewel."

Rosie did so. Immediately, rainbow colours radiated around the star, and the blue central gem shimmered with the occasional flash of a pure fluorescent blue light.

"It's now tied genetically to you and your motivator, invisibly linked across the galaxy. Here, let me put it on for you." He carefully lifted the jewel and passed the fine gold chain over her head. The star sat comfortably at the base of her neck radiating a cultured glow. "It's called the 'Star of Alcyone'. It represents the Goddess, the blue star. One of the seven sisters of our Pleiades star cluster. May she always protect you."

"I don't know what to say," said Rosie. "It's the most beautiful thing I've ever seen." She could feel the necklace, an almost imperceptible yet warm electric current ever so slightly reacting with her skin. "Does it contain some of the motivator crystal?"

"It does," said Titania. "It will allow you to leave your motivator box safely locked away. The jewel contains only a small fraction of the power of a motivator. You can wear it safely, and it will help in translation as you walk on our world."

"Thank you," said Rosie. "I feel a little overwhelmed."

Titania and Alannah started to prepare some food at the other end of the kitchen.

Rosie approached Thumblerock. "Can I have a word with you, Rocky?"

"Of course. What's the matter?"

"I don't know what it means, but we found some footprints on the beach by the lake. It looked like they came from two Trolls and a human." Thumblerock's jaw dropped as the words hit home. "We followed the prints for about a kilometre when they stopped at the boat jetty. We could see a small boat moored at the other side of the lake; they must have crossed over."

"Are you absolutely sure, Rosie?"

"Yes, but as it's been raining, I'm worried the prints will have been washed away before you can see them. Can you ask Hattie and Quizzical to confirm my story?"

"Yes, yes, come on," he said. "Hattie! Atlas! You need to hear this." They all left the kitchen and headed to the barn.

"What's going on?" asked Atlas as he hurried behind Thumblerock, who was striding across the yard.

"Rosie thinks she has seen some human boot prints next to a couple of Troll prints down by the lakeside. I just want to hear from Quizzical and Hattie. A corroborated story is always much better for all concerned."

"Wow," said Atlas. "I can understand your concern."

Rosie sat on a hay bale as Thumblerock and Atlas conversed with both Hattie and Quizzical. She couldn't make anything of the conversation, but a worried look on Thumblerock's face obviously confirmed her story.

Thumblerock came across to Rosie as Atlas began rubbing down Quizzical with a horse brush. "Both have verified your story in their own way," he said. "The most worrying is Hattie – she recognised the human scent within the prints." He then added, "Right, at daybreak tomorrow, Atlas, Hattie, Quizzical and I will go back to the lake and try to follow the trail. We have other boats there, so we can have a look over on the other side. There's nothing more we can do tonight."

Titania was calling them. "Come on, we have food prepared for everyone," she shouted. "Don't let it go cold."

As they returned to the house, Thumblerock let the others know what was going on. Everyone seemed a little shocked.

"I suggest we keep it to ourselves," he said. "After we've investigated, I'll need to report my findings to the Council. Rosie, we have to leave tomorrow afternoon anyway for Sculptor and your Council meeting. As soon as Atlas and I return from the lake."

"Can Celaeno come to the city with us?" asked Rosie.

"Well, I don't know," said Thumblerock, caught a little off guard.

"I think that's a good idea," said Atlas. "Titania should go along, too, and take the girls around the city. I expect your business with the Council may take a little extra time in light of these new developments." Thumblerock nodded a little hesitantly.

So, it was agreed that Thumblerock, Rosie, Celaeno and her mother, Titania, would be journeying to Sculptor, the Central Domain, perhaps as early as tomorrow afternoon.

They spent the evening as friends sitting around the table eating, drinking and telling stories. Celaeno took Rosie to her room to have some non-adult time, which Rosie enjoyed immensely. All too soon, they needed to leave.

Rosie, Thumblerock and Alannah climbed into the cart, and they rolled quietly out of the farm, thanking each other for a pleasant evening.

Hattie was staying in the barn with Quizzical overnight. She was pooped after the day's exercise. She would accompany Atlas and Quizzical at dawn to meet with Thumblerock by the lake. Standing in the barn door, she watched them roll away.

"Bye, Hattie," Rosie shouted.

She barked once, turned around and went back inside.

Atlas was back in the barn early the next morning to prepare. He fed Hattie some biscuits and spoke to them both. "Can you take me back to the lakeside where you first started following the footprints?"

Hattie barked and Quizzical snorted. They left the farm in the direction of the lake.

At the same time, Thumblerock was with Ceres trotting down the country lane to meet them.

The sun was just about waking, enough light to navigate by as Thumblerock brooded over the situation. He was worried; he couldn't figure out how another human could be on his planet other than Rosie. The motivators Thumblerock and Rosie used were more sophisticated than the power sources of the general population. They contained the ability to manipulate space, to travel between worlds. They weren't easy to get hold of, and all travel was person specific. Something clearly wasn't right.

He needed to be careful in the capital. He had a trustworthy close friend whom he would seek out before meeting with the Council.

Atlas suggesting the other ladies should come along was turning out to be a sensible solution. It would give him time to meet with his colleagues without trawling Rosie around. The last thing he wanted was to expose her to a potentially dangerous situation.

He and Alannah were becoming attached to Rosie in the short time she'd been with them. He thought of her as the daughter they'd never had. No one was going to put her at risk in any way; he would make sure of that. She'd already proved how intelligent and perceptive she was. Saving a young Troll's life in the heat of the moment and now discovering an oddity. Footprints on the beach that didn't make sense to her. Most individuals wouldn't have even noticed.

In his pocket, Thumblerock carried a small weapon, a handgun of sorts, powered by a tiny motivator crystal. In certain circumstances he would carry it, if he thought it was justified. This situation warranted it. He would protect his charge and his close friend Atlas, should that become necessary.

Once he'd joined with Atlas, Hattie and Quizzical at the bottom of the hill near the lake, they rode side by side discussing the situation. When they reached the beginning of the tracks, Hattie barked and started sniffing. The outline of the boots Rosie saw yesterday were now undefined, although Hattie could still pick out the faint scent. They followed her to the boat jetty. They could still see the small boat tied up on the other side of the lake.

"I'll bring another boat around," said Atlas. He walked off over a small hill. On the other side was a hut suspended over the water. He went inside and jumped into a small boat, then plugged in his motivator and silently swept out and around the corner to the jetty where Thumblerock was talking to the horses.

He turned and jumped in with Hattie close behind. She was a little hesitant but followed him onto the boat. She wasn't totally sure about it, so sat nervously in the middle getting in the way.

"Come on, Hattie," said Thumblerock. "Move up to the front so we can all sit down."

Hattie grumbled, then crept forward onto the front flat board and stared out across the lake.

The horses turned and walked away to find some grass to eat. They would wait a while for their return. If the delay were too long, Thumblerock would send them a message by a bird so they could return to the farm. Thumblerock had another communication device if he needed to speak with Alannah, but this was no use with the animals.

The little boat left the jetty and picked up speed as it moved out across the lake. Only the sound of the water being parted by the hull could be heard. Hattie faced the wind with her ears flapping in the breeze. She watched the wildlife up and down the lake. Some ducks and swans complained as the boat's speed made them paddle faster to get out of the way. Atlas was apologising to them. Hattie thought that their reaction was a bit rude – they were shouting fowl obscenities as the boat passed by.

Now focused on the jetty on the opposite side, which was approaching fast, she was looking forward to jumping off the boat and trying to pick up the human scent. She was totally committed to her task and didn't want to let Thumblerock down. He'd asked her the previous evening if she wanted Taurus the Collie to come along and help. She declined and told him that she knew the human scent so well after living with them for many years. Taurus would probably distract her.

"I'm going to miss you when you go home," said Thumblerock with a chuckle.

The boat gently nudged the jetty, and Hattie leapt off and ran to the edge of the forest track. She roamed around until she was sure she'd picked up the correct scent. She barked.

Thumblerock and Atlas tied up the boat and followed her between the trees. Ahead of them was a trail, which wound through the forest as it rose towards the foothills of a distant mountain range. They knew the area well having been brought up here and roaming around as youngsters.

Atlas knew Thumblerock's role with the Council was sometimes mysterious and secret. He was always available to help and support his friend when asked. He worried for his friend when he travelled, being so closely involved in the politics of worlds. It was always going to be a hazardous occupation.

"I think I know where they're heading," said Atlas. "The old unused portal at Mount Ahuna."

Nodding, Thumblerock said, "I was having the same thoughts. That mountain is two days' walk from here, and they have at least a day's head start."

"Yes," said Atlas. "It would be the ideal way off the planet without much chance of being noticed. I thought that portal was decommissioned?"

"Me too," said Thumblerock. "Let's just walk as far as the path separation. If Hattie shows us that they are heading for the mountain, then we'll know for sure. I just don't have the time to follow them all the way into the mountains."

They walked for another two hours with Hattie leading the way. The climb was getting more and more difficult; she was struggling, slowing down and panting. It was mid-morning and hot in the starlight.

"Not far now, Hattie," said Thumblerock. "Just over that ridge and the path will separate into two. We will rest there."

Hattie charged ahead with renewed vigour; she arrived at a junction just over the rise. One path curved around to the west and the other route led north, further into the foothills of the mountains ahead. Hattie lay down in the direction of this path, pointing to where the scent trail led and waited for them to catch up.

"So now we know," said Thumblerock, as they came over the top of the ridge and saw Hattie. "They're heading for the old portal. Well done, Hattie. We'll take a short rest here, and then we must return to the lake."

Thumblerock gave Hattie a good scratch when she wandered over and produced a chew from his pocket.

It was much easier returning to the lake, pretty much downhill all the way. Hattie, now that she was off duty, ran in and out of the trees and scrub chasing smells and looking for anything interesting to eat. It was whilst she was in a thicket that she started barking and came out with a drink can in her mouth. She immediately took it to Atlas who stopped to wait for her.

"Man, water," is all she said to him before walking on.

Atlas shouted to Thumblerock who was a little way ahead, "Rocky, take a look at this. Hattie's just found it."

Thumblerock ran up to him puffing a little and took the can from Atlas. "Well, that just about seals it," he said. "I now have some hard evidence that we have another human on Damianos. Thanks, old girl. If you hadn't been here with us, we'd never have found this. Well done." He pulled out another dog chew and gave it to her.

"Thanks," said Hattie.

They arrived back at the lake around midday.

"Let's take both the boats back to the boathouse on the other side," said Thumblerock. "If we assume they'll come back this way, I don't want to make life easy for them."

So off they went, Hattie and Thumblerock in one and Atlas in the other boat. The horses were still waiting, and met them at the jetty.

"We need to get back to the farm as quick as you can?" said Thumblerock to Quizzical and Ceres.

They mounted the horses and took off at a pace. Hattie ran behind them as fast as she could along the shore, up through the big gate and through the low path between the fields.

When they arrived in the yard, all the animals went for a cooling drink from a trough. Hattie sloped off into the barn and found some straw to stretch out and sleep – she was exhausted. Atlas and Thumblerock were in conference discussing arrangements for the trip to Sculptor.

Atlas was to take a carriage back to their farm, help Titania and Celaeno prepare for the journey, and then return with them as soon as possible. Alannah and Atlas would look after the farms, the animals and the injured Callisto whilst they were away. Atlas was also going to keep watch on the lakeside for the return of the Trolls and human, should that happen. He would enlist some help from the forest animals to report any unusual visitors to the area, especially the owls and crows; they were the more intelligent creatures and understood the importance of not being noticed. They hoped the removal of the boat would just be considered a nuisance to these intruders. It would also redirect them to a lengthy detour around the lake, making it much easier for anyone watching to follow their movements.

Chapter 7 Sculptor – The Central Domain

Thumblerock was sitting at the kitchen table with Rosie and Alannah telling them what had happened that morning. He produced the drinks can from his pocket, to which Rosie gasped.

"Coke. Well, that's definitely not from here, is it?" she said.

"No, no, it isn't," said Thumblerock. "Hattie found it in some bushes just off the path. She's a clever girl she is – just the proof we need to back up your story." He added, "As soon as Titania and Celaeno arrive, we need to leave. That should put us in Sculptor this evening."

"Come on, Rosie, let's go and pack a bag," said Alannah. "I expect you'll be away for a day or two."

Thumblerock left them to it and went to gather the belongings he would need. Afterwards, he went into the yard to see to the animals. He asked Quizzical to take him to the locus to collect a carriage for their trip, and off they went.

"I'm really looking forward to seeing the city," said Rosie. "What's it like, Alannah?"

"I assume you have cities on your world so probably quite similar, with lots of people bustling about. It's different from life on the farm."

Rosie looked a little concerned. "On the other hand," she said, "I'm worried about seeing the Council."

"Try not to think about it so much and don't worry. With these recent developments, I expect they're going to be a little distracted."

Alannah was trying to keep the atmosphere between them light and uncomplicated. She knew Rosie was worrying about so many things. It was a lot to ask a young girl to cope with, and she'd performed admirably so far.

"I've packed some nightclothes, a few blouses and trousers. You will have to take your boots, as we don't have any shoes in your size. I'll take good care of Hattie. I suggest you go and say goodbye. She was in the barn snoozing the last time I saw her."

Rosie carried her bag down and left it in the kitchen, then walked across the yard towards the barn. Hattie was snoring loudly in the pig pen with her head resting on a large pink pig called Bunting. She raised her head as she approached. As Rosie knelt beside her, Hattie licked her hand.

"Hello, Hattie, you look as though you've been busy. I've just come to say goodbye. We are travelling for a few days, and I want you to stay here with Alannah on the farm. We're going to the city you see, and it will just be too busy for you. I hope you understand?"

Hattie stood up and pushed her head between Rosie's arm and side, completely burying her head.

Just then, Rosie heard a cart roll into the yard. "That will be the others. I'll have to go. I know Rocky is in a hurry to get away."

Hattie grumbled and returned to the pen with Bunting. She turned around and barked once as Rosie left the barn.

In the yard were two carts: the farm cart, which Atlas, Titania, Celaeno and Callisto had arrived in; and just behind them, Thumblerock arrived with the carriage from the locus, for their trip to the city. As all the adults rushed about arranging things, Rosie joined Celaeno and Callisto in the farm cart.

"How are you feeling today, Callisto?" asked Rosie.

"Oh, much better thanks. I wish I were coming with you – I so love the city. If I hadn't fallen into that stupid fish slide?"

Celaeno laughed. "Well, that's your own fault. It could have been much worse."

"I know, I know," he said. "Have a great time, Rosie, and don't worry about the stupid Council." Rosie smiled and put her hand on his arm.

"We'll bring you something back, a surprise if we can."

"Oh yes, please, that would be great," he said.

"Come on, Rosie, Celaeno. We're ready to go," said Thumblerock.

They all jumped down from the farm cart and walked to the more luxurious carriage. Atlas placed all the bags in the storage locker for them and helped Rosie up to her seat. He hugged Titania and Celaeno, and they joined Rosie. Thumblerock was talking to Alannah, holding her hands as she looked a little distressed. After they kissed, he let go. Atlas then put his arm around her for comfort as Thumblerock boarded the carriage. It rolled slowly out of the yard. Alannah, Atlas and Callisto waved until they were out of sight.

Thumblerock smiled at Rosie. "Make yourself comfortable, ladies. We're off to the portal. It's the same one where we arrived at Rosie, in the large tree a few days ago."

She nodded. "How far is Sculptor?"

"Well, it's located on a different continent on the west side of the planet. We should be there early evening all being well. I've booked some rooms at a lovely old inn near the city centre."

"Are we staying at the Asterope Inn?" asked Celaeno.

"We are," he said.

"Wow," said Celaeno. "You'll really love it, Rosie. I've always wanted to stay there, and it's right in the centre near all the entertainment and nightlife. Will you take us to see a performance, Titania?" she asked her mother.

Thumblerock nodded his head and added, "I want you to take Rosie to see as much of our city as you can. The Council have said they will pay the bills."

"Wonderful," said Titania.

Celaeno was whooping. "This is going to be great," she said.

The carriage rolled comfortably along the road towards the portal. The sun was starting to drop down below the black hills creating a fabulous orange sunset. It was quiet with few other carriages or carts on the road, just rolling farmland and occasional dwellings with lights flickering on here and there. *So peaceful*, thought Rosie, *compared to the roads at home with cars and lorries charging about*. She sensed that her time here was approaching its end. Rosie was looking forward to going home but also sad because she would have to leave soon.

Not long after she must have fallen asleep, as the carriage had now stopped.

"Come on, Rosie," said Celaeno. "We've arrived."

Rosie climbed down as far as she could, with Celaeno helping her off the final step. Thumblerock lifted out all the bags, and the carriage then reversed itself into the locus, ready for its next customer.

They walked up the slight rise through the trees, now lit by a row of beautiful rainbow-coloured lanterns strung out above the path. There it was – the entrance in the tree. The door was pulled open by Thumblerock; Titania led the way down a few short steps to a platform. Above them, the roof was glowing in wondrous colourful waves.

"Has everyone got their motivators in the palm of their hands?" asked Thumblerock.

Rosie put her hand in her coat pocket and closed it around the little silver box. She could feel the gentle static pricking through her fingers.

Once they'd all looped their arms together, Thumblerock whispered quietly, "Sculptor Central."

An instant blinding flash of colour erupted all around them. Rosie could feel a rush of static and no ground beneath her. Rather than keeping her eyes open, she closed them tightly, this time in the hope that she would not feel so nauseous at the other end.

Within seconds, her feet were firmly planted once again. She opened her eyes to reveal that she was standing in a glass dome with just enough room for them all. Through the glass, she could see crystal buildings towering all around and lit up with waves of magical colour.

Thumblerock opened the door, and they stepped out into a frosty evening breeze. It was cold here. Trolls of all sizes were walking in different directions, all buttoned up in their overcoats. She could see behind her a row of glass domes, the one they had just stepped out of included. This was obviously a travel hub with people coming in or leaving the city. Each dome flashed regularly; people appeared and disappeared in a colourful instant.

Rosie walked next to Celaeno, following Thumblerock and Titania as they strode across a plaza.

"Hey, you two," shouted Celaeno, "Rosie can't keep up this pace. Slow down."

"Of course, Rosie, I'm sorry," said Thumblerock. "The inn is not too far from here."

They slowed to a more comfortable pace for Rosie, who grasped onto Celaeno's hand. She didn't want to get lost or separated; there were a lot of Trolls walking all around her.

Some who noticed her stared, looking back as they passed. It didn't seem quite so friendly as the countryside they'd come from. A similar feeling to being on Earth and walking in a town or city you're not familiar with.

Passing through an outdoor market with food being prepared on little stoves, they saw customers sat around on stools chatting and enjoying the evening. The high-rise buildings all around the plaza were shimmering. It looked as though they were made of glass, with a frosted icy look. You couldn't see through, however; the lights shone from inside. The overall appearance was very impressive. They all shimmered in the cold air radiating their own personal rainbows.

They were approaching some dark glass doors that were fixed at an angle and rising out of the pavement. As they neared, they swished open. Inside, an elevator disappeared underground. It was encompassed in a glass tube with various shades of green vegetation wrapped all around. The light filtered through, making their progress seem as if they were floating along a jungle path.

Then the scene changed, which startled Rosie. It was like she was falling. A 360-degree, three-dimensional view of Damianos appeared all around the escalator. The scene then retreated from the planet into space. It showed a view of the galaxy with faint cords of light connecting different planets in all directions.

It then picked one cord and followed it to a distant planet. Soaring at flight level over the plains of the planet, it showed the topography, a glimpse of culture, and the inhabitants standing side by side with Trolls. The view then repeated along a cord to a different world, and then another, again and again, visiting worlds across the galaxy.

Rosie was gobsmacked; these were obviously other civilisations at a similar level of development to the Trolls.

The view then changed again. It followed various cords to other worlds, but only showed the planets spinning in the black of space. Then it arrived at Earth in the same way. Rosie started to cry; her world was rotated in its deep beautiful blue. It looked so peaceful. It was home.

The picture now retreated to follow another trail. Rosie understood the meaning instantly. The Earth was one of a few developing worlds significantly behind in its technology and cultural development. She realised she already knew this; however, it was still a shock to see that we were classed as a third-division society. It made her feel a little ashamed.

At the bottom of the escalator, the space opened out to reveal a large foyer. The visual display was over. A large wooden frontage appeared in front of them, a bit like an old western saloon entrance with authentic swing doors. It was glazed with picture windows and colourful lights shining through from the inside. It looked welcoming. A semicircle sign was suspended above the doors on a chain saying “Asterope Inn”.

Thumblerock pushed through one of the doors and held it open for everyone to pass through. They approached the reception counter; it was so tall that Rosie was completely hidden from view. She could hear Thumblerock speaking with the receptionist and getting the keys for the rooms. A large, curious face peered over the counter and looked down at her. It didn’t smile; instead, it just studied her for a moment, then the face disappeared. Rosie was a little unnerved.

“Who was that?” she whispered to Celaeno.

“The hotel manager or a receptionist I think,” she replied.

“He looks jolly,” she said, and Celaeno giggled.

Off to their rooms they went, with a young male Troll carrying as many bags as he could. He kept looking round at Rosie.

After the third time, she said, “What?” and pushed her chin out in defiance.

He looked away, a little embarrassed.

The hotel was grand with ornate carvings and beautiful tapestries covering the walls. Thick blue carpets trimmed with red ran along the edge of each corridor. Others branched off at various angles from the main walkway; she could see doors each side with room numbers on them. There didn’t appear to be any stairs or escalators. The whole hotel seemed to be on one underground level.

They took one of these corridors and walked past a dozen rooms before the concierge stopped and opened the first door.

“This room is for us,” said Titania. “Rocky is just opposite.”

Thumblerock tipped the boy a coin, and he left. Their room contained a large bed and a slightly smaller one. When you say large, it was easily twice the size of any bed Rosie had ever seen. There was a dressing table, some built-in wardrobes and a bathroom running off the far end. The ceiling seemed to be made of that frosted crystal, as she could see the city lights shining through.

“Watch this,” said Celaeno. She turned a dial on the wall and the frosted ceiling became completely transparent. She could see the city in all its splendour shining in the night sky.

“Cool,” said Rosie. “Can anyone out there see us?”

“No, they can’t, so don’t worry. That word you used, ‘cool’, what does it mean?”

“Oh, just like really amazing or surprising I guess.”

"I love it," said Celaeno. "The words you use, it's so entertaining. You need to teach me some more." She turned the dial the other way, and the glass became completely opaque and black.

"Neat," said Rosie. Celaeno giggled again.

Titania came into the room; she'd been speaking with Thumblerock. "Okay, you two take the large bed. You don't mind do you, Rosie?"

"Not at all, it will be fun," she said. "The size of it, you probably won't notice I'm in there. In fact, you're going to have to help me to get into it later, otherwise I'll have to take a running jump."

Celaeno and Titania burst out laughing. "We're going to miss you when you leave, Rosie," said Celaeno.

"I feel the same way," she said. "Let's not think about it for now."

"Good idea," said Titania, realising too late that it wasn't very tactful. "Rocky has some appointments this evening, so it's just the three of us going out for dinner. Where do you suggest we go, Celaeno? I'm sure you'll want to show Rosie somewhere the young and trendy might go."

"I can think of a few 'cool' places," said Celaeno, laughing.

Titania smiled and looked a little confused. "One of Rosie's expressions I expect."

"Yes, it's really 'neat', isn't it?" said Celaeno, trying to keep a straight face. Then they all fell about laughing. "Let's go to the restaurant overlooking the river. They have live musicians playing the latest songs and the views are wonderful. I think it's called the Prickly Fish or something?"

"I'll call reception and ask them to book us a table," said Titania.

About an hour later, they were all changed and refreshed. The three of them left the inn by the escalator once more. This time the views showing on their trip up to the plaza were a lot less disturbing for Rosie. They concentrated on all the beautiful landscapes of Damianos. Mountains, islands, waterfalls, even beaches – a bit like a holiday advert from Earth. They showed families at leisure or working on farms together with animals. The cities were highlighted showing fascinating buildings combined with technologies she didn't quite understand. Also, structures leading straight upwards through the clouds and into space with carriages gliding along them.

They passed through the escalator doors. Rosie walked between them holding hands with Celaeno. It was busy and quite chilly, and she was still attracting a lot of attention.

"Just ignore them," said Celaeno. "People are just ignorant; they will always stare at anyone who is different or unusual."

"It's the same on Earth," said Rosie. "I thought your society would be more enlightened?"

"For the most part they are," said Titania. "However, the general population rarely think about anything other than their own little lives. They don't see many off-worlders actually walking through the city. Few of us travel off-world, so you're a curiosity here."

The paths they were walking along were internally lit. Directions and arrows pointed here and there within the pavements, showing the way to various selected destinations. Rosie was fascinated.

"What do the symbols mean?" she asked Celaeno.

"We have symbols for just about everything. That one is for a market, that one is for medical facilities, and over there to various transport hubs. They are repeated regularly so people can easily find their way. You can also borrow a handheld device from the hotel or information centres and plan in all your destinations. The routes will be displayed along the path in front of you as you walk."

"We have similar systems on Earth called 'satellite navigation'," said Rosie. "Although, they are not nearly as sophisticated."

They arrived at the river and walked along a raised pathway. A few hardy individuals were in boats paddling up and down enjoying the evening. Numerous restaurants and bars welcomed customers by boat as well as on foot.

"That's where we're going," said Celaeno. She pointed to a building with a bamboo façade, extending out above the river. It had banners of different colours swaying underneath in the breeze.

Rosie could see Trolls sat at tables eating and drinking. They were lit by up rainbow-coloured lanterns, and she could hear soft music floating in the air.

They were greeted at the door by a young male Troll in a colourful uniform. He led them to a table in the overhang above the river. Celaeno helped Rosie onto her seat. She could just about see the river view over the top of the surrounding bamboo wall.

The Troll introduced himself as Rigel. He said he would be attending to their requirements this evening and asked if he could bring some drinks as they looked through the menus.

Titania ordered for them as Celaeno was blushing.

"You think he's cute, Celaeno?" asked Rosie. She giggled as he left the table.

"Quiet, Rosie, stop it now." Celaeno turned even redder.

A jug of iced juice arrived accompanied by beautifully crafted glass goblets. Rigel also produced a much smaller version.

"For the little lady," he said, and smiled as he placed the goblet in front of her.

"Thank you, Rigel, how kind."

"It's a pleasure to have you here with us," he said before backing away from the table.

"Well, I've got no chance, have I?" said Celaeno, laughing.

Thumblerock was walking through the side streets in the south side of the city. He'd arranged to meet another Troll who he'd known since his training days before embarking on his role with the Council. His name was Tauri, and Thumblerock trusted him implicitly. He wanted to talk through the events of the last few days and get his perspective before his meeting with the Council.

He strolled down a narrow cobbled street, arrived at a door and knocked. He could hear footsteps approaching and the door swung open.

"Rocky, hello, it's so good to see you. Come in from the cold." He let Thumblerock pass and then popped his head out to check up and down the street. All seemed quiet. He closed and locked the door and followed Thumblerock. "Just go straight to the front room. I'll take your coat."

It was a small house but pleasantly decorated in a Victorian style. Lots of wooden panels, pictures on the walls and thick drapes around each window. Two chairs were arranged at either side of a roaring rainbow fire. The room was dimly lit and comfortable. Once Thumblerock and Tauri sat down facing each other, Tauri poured a small glass of spirit for each of them.

"It's good to see you, old friend," said Thumblerock. "Is everything all right with you and your work?"

"For the most part," said Tauri. "Although, I sense a change in the wind. There seems to be too many secrets and whispers in the corridors of power. I was not surprised to hear from you. I was about to ask you for a meet – you've beaten me to it. Tell me of your concerns."

Gripping his glass, Thumblerock looked anxiously at his friend. "As you know, I have my charge, Rosie, visiting from Earth. I was asked to contact her and bring her here so we can close the Earth gate. We know why... She's a clever girl, perceptive and courageous. Similar in fact to her great-grandfather, although a lot more cautious. A few days with us, and she has already created quite a stir in the community. She undoubtedly saved the life of my neighbours' youngster Callisto."

"Yes," said Tauri. "I heard about that. Come now, Rocky, there must be more. Tell me what's worrying you."

Thumblerock started again, "Rosie was out on her own the other day with Quizzical and Hattie, her dog. A real character, by the way, and has proved damn useful. Whilst walking by Lake Veyatie near the farm, Rosie noticed some tracks on the beach. Two Trolls and a set of human boot prints." Tauri sat up immediately.

"How can that be? She must be mistaken?"

"I agree it sounds ridiculous, but both Quizzical and Hattie backed up her story. The Earth dog even confirmed the human scent." Tauri slumped back in his chair. Thumblerock continued with his story. "The following day, Atlas, Hattie and I retraced their steps. The tracks in the sand were mostly washed away by the overnight rain. We crossed over the lake, the direction we assumed they'd taken, and the Earth dog picked up the scent again. We followed the trail up over the foothills to the break in the path. The scent indicated that they were heading towards the old portal on Mount Ahuna. As the tracks were at least a day old, I decided we should return to the lake. The Council needed to be informed, and I had to bring Rosie to the Council meeting anyway." His friend considered the story so far.

"It's just not credible, Rocky. If you go to the Council with hearsay evidence of Rosie and her dog, they will just dismiss it. You must realise that?"

"Knowing Rosie and Hattie as I do, I was convinced by their evidence and prepared to go to the Council on the strength of it. However, that's not all." Thumblerock went out to where his coat was hanging and fished in the pocket. He pulled out the drink can, walked back into the room and handed it to Tauri. "Found in a thicket by Hattie just off the path on our return to the lake."

Tauri was gobsmacked. "This is just unbelievable." He examined the can and looked at the printing around it.

"Rosie confirmed it's a popular Earth drink. There's no mistaking what she called the 'brand name'."

Sitting back once again and considering all that his old friend had said and shown him, Tauri poured them both another glass. "You must not present this evidence to the full Council," he said. "As I mentioned earlier, I've been concerned about some of the members these past few months. There's something going on, and this evidence of yours just heightens my suspicions. No, Rocky, you must go straight to the Secretary. It's up to her to decide the next steps."

Thumblerock nodded. "You're right, Tauri. I'm glad of your advice. I was concerned about telling them all. Some of them must be involved – I can't see any other explanation. How can we have two travellers from Earth here at the same time? I must find out what's going on. I'm concerned for Rosie's safety, as this has major implications for her. I'm due to take her to the General Council meeting tomorrow so they can discuss the closure of the gate. Where does that leave us now?"

"I know this really complicates things," said Tauri. "You must take great care, and let me know if I can help in any way."

Chapter 8 Private Investigations

Rosie ordered some fish with vegetables in a spicy sauce; it was wonderfully tasty. Whilst they were eating, a musician played a strange-looking stringed instrument. It was shaped like a box, and he played each side by spinning it around. Each panel resonated with a completely different range of sounds. It was magical.

They chatted and laughed all through the evening. The young waiter was attentive; he seemed star-struck with Rosie.

Finishing the meal with a selection of sweet pastries, the night was winding down. There was a steady flow of people leaving the restaurant and a few tables around them were now empty. Thumblerock strode in, spotted them and took a seat at their table. Titania sensed an air of tension behind his eyes.

"Girls," she said, "it's been a long day. I think we need to return to the hotel for some rest. You have a big day tomorrow, Rosie. We don't want you falling asleep in front of the Council."

"What will happen tomorrow, Rocky?" asked Rosie.

"Well, we'll leave the hotel after breakfast and travel to the Central Council building. I have an appointment first, then we'll have to wait, I expect, until they're ready to meet with you. I will accompany you so don't fret; we should be finished with them by midday or early afternoon. We can meet up with Titania and Celaeno for a little sightseeing if you like?"

"Can we go to the theatre tomorrow night?" asked Celaeno.

"Yes, yes, I suppose so," he said. "It will be our last night in the city, as we need to leave for home the following morning." Thumblerock took a glass of fruit juice from the jug and drank it thirstily.

As they all got up to leave, the young waiter hurried over and asked if they'd enjoyed their evening.

"It was lovely, thank you, Rigel," said Rosie. "Thank you for serving us so well." Rigel now blushed.

"It was my honour." He presented Rosie, Celaeno and Titania with a beautiful fluorescent orange flower in a thin, frosted crystal flute.

Thumblerock raised his eyebrows to Titania, unseen by Rosie. "I see you've made another good impression, Rosie," he said. They all laughed as they left the restaurant.

It was a chilly walk back to the hotel, although not so far thankfully, as the cold wind made its presence felt. Once Thumblerock swung open the weird, angled doors, they all joined the escalator for the ride down to the hotel entrance. Rosie was thankful; it was just more fabulous scenery and some advertising of attractions around the city.

"Rocky," she asked, "the visual display on the escalator, the first time we descended to the hotel, it showed all the planets and concentrated on the Earth? It was quite upsetting in a way."

"Each of us will see a completely different view. The scene will reflect something that's on your mind or troubling your subconscious. I expect it answered some questions you had?"

"It did, Rocky, in quite a brutal way."

"Your mind needed answers. It just helps to rationalise your thoughts."

Once back in the room, Celaeno showed Rosie another use of the crystal ceiling. When she activated a panel by the bed, pictures spread across it like a cinema screen. Each area was displaying a different subject: one was a news feed, some sporting highlights and various other public interest channels.

"It's much like television back home," said Rosie. "Do you have this in your home as well?"

"We do," said Celaeno. "It's more for educational use and as a teaching aid in school."

"We have television channels for just about everything," said Rosie. "Mostly for entertainment; in fact, humans watch far too much of it."

"Oh," said Celaeno, a little confused. "No, we don't have that."

"Celaeno, you mentioned going to the theatre tomorrow night?"

"Oh yes, I hope we can. It's popular here. The actors put on some amazing shows. Sometimes there will be historical dramas or perhaps stories from other worlds. Let's have a look and see what's on." Celaeno touched the panel on the wall, and the theatre listings appeared on the crystal screen above their heads. They both lay back on the bed while Celaeno explained the choices being displayed.

She went through the various options covering historical events or the latest popular shows. Rosie didn't really have enough knowledge of this planet to make an informed decision. One suddenly appeared which sparked her interest. It was called *Damianos and the Motivator Crystal*.

"What about that one?" she said. "Perhaps it will help me to make a little more sense of your beautiful world." Celaeno turned to Rosie.

"I can understand why you would want to see it. I can't imagine how hard it's been for you to try and adjust to our way of life."

Titania and Thumblerock came into the room; they'd been discussing tomorrow's arrangements.

"Rosie would like to go and see this performance tomorrow night." Celaeno pointed at the screen. "Can we take her?" They both looked up, and Thumblerock looked a little surprised. Titania turned to him.

"I think it's an excellent idea. It will give her much more of an insight into what our ancestors went through, the reason she is here and why contact is made this way."

"Of course," said Thumblerock. "Why am I not surprised?" He smiled at her. "If all the young people of Earth are anything like you, Rosie, I believe your planet will be in good hands. Could you organise the tickets, Titania? I must go out for a short while. I wish you all a good night," he said before leaving the room.

Thumblerock left the hotel and headed straight for the portal. He'd received a message from Atlas – the sort of message that suggested they should meet in person.

He stepped onto the escalator, then strode quickly across the plaza. He entered one of the glass domes and spoke softly. A flash of colour and less than a minute later, he was making his way down the path from the old oak tree, towards the locus.

It was the following afternoon on this continent, so a considerable period of time, almost eighteen hours, had passed since they'd left for the city. He went inside and boarded a carriage at the far end. Atlas was sat waiting for him.

"Hello, old friend, tell me what news?"

Atlas began. "Not long after you left, just around midnight, I received a message from the owls. There was activity at the head of the pass. Two Trolls were seen returning along the Mount Ahuna trail and heading down towards the lake. They were carrying a large black case between them, and it seemed heavy. I reckoned I had time to get down there to see what they were up to. I went with Quizzical and Hattie of course, as I thought she would be useful. There was a full moon, so I dressed all in black. Hattie and Quizzical were already in disguise." He laughed at his little joke. "We stopped at the foot of the path by the big gate for cover, and I watched the jetty across the lake with my spyglass. Soon enough, they appeared. I could hear them shouting obscenities when they realised the boat was no longer there. There was much stamping about and muttering. The weight of the box they were carrying was obviously quite a problem. You won't believe this, Rocky, but I watched them bury it, a good distance from the jetty and well off the trail."

"Good, good. Go on," said Thumblerock.

"Well, once they were satisfied they'd hidden the box, they made their way south along the lakeside, heading towards the village. I sat and thought about the situation. What was in the box? Who were they? And where were they going? So, Hattie and I came up with a plan. She would follow the Trolls from this side of the lake and onwards until they arrived at their destination, or as far as she could sensibly go. She would then return to my farm. There was little chance of her being seen in the darkness and she's so quiet."

Nodding, Thumblerock whistled between his teeth before saying, "Good old Hattie."

Atlas continued, "Once they were out of sight, I took a boat across the lake to investigate the box. Quizzical would wait for my return, and we would all meet back at the farm."

"Is Hattie okay?" asked Thumblerock.

"Oh yes, just completely exhausted, it was a long night for her. She said she'll be glad to get back home – too much charging about on this world." Thumblerock smiled. Atlas carried on with his account, "I went straight across the lake and quickly found where the box was buried and dug it up. Rocky, it was full of Earth weapons, all expertly packed as if straight from an armoury."

Thumblerock whistled again. He knew Atlas would tell his story at his own pace, but he was feeling a little frustrated.

"Well," said Atlas, "I needed to make a quick decision, so I removed all the weapons from the box and brought them back over in the boat. I've hidden them in some sacking under the boathouse. I refilled the box with stones and wood, all packed tight, and reburied it. Hopefully when they return for it, they won't check it."

"You've done well, Atlas. I'd have done the same thing, but what of Hattie?"

"Okay, I returned to the farm with Quizzical and waited in the barn all night. I couldn't sleep; I was sick with worry. It was dawn before she crept into the stable and collapsed with exhaustion. She told me that she could lead me back to the place where they had stopped. She said, 'Was plenty far,' in her manner of speaking. So I fed her and let her sleep for a few hours. Then, about mid-morning, the three of us set off again in the cart. Quizzical insisted on taking it so Hattie could fully recover. We went well beyond the village up towards Lake Elgol and the old, abandoned mining cottages."

After whistling once more, Thumblerock said, "Must be four miles at least from your farm. It's quiet up there. You weren't seen, were you?"

"No, I realised where we were heading so stopped before the cottages came into view. I crept to a vantage point and used my spyglass. Sure enough, one of the abandoned cottages was inhabited – it was them. I recognised one of the Troll's clothing from the previous night. So we turned around and hurried back as fast as Quizzical could go. Oh, and I've brought this for you." Atlas stretched for his bag and produced a sackcloth parcel, which he passed to his friend.

Once Thumblerock had unwrapped it, he studied the contents. There was an Earth weapon and another small black box. He carefully lifted the lid of the black box. Inside were four silver motivator boxes, which he recognised immediately. As he lifted one out, it started to radiate colour, sending a tingle through his hand. Thumblerock was stunned; he looked up at Atlas.

"How can this be? How can it activate without my genome recognition?"

Atlas shrugged his shoulders.

"You've done well, my friend; this is indeed a significant mystery. Return home and be safe. Ask the lookouts to continue to monitor the lake and report to you. Do not go back there – promise me, Atlas. I've put you in enough danger. I'll be back early the day after tomorrow. Pass my regards to Hattie and Quizzical. I'm proud of them both." Thumblerock jumped out of the carriage, and then waved to his friend as it rolled away with Atlas towards home.

He walked back up to the large tree, through the door and down the steps to the portal platform. In an instant, he was back in the city centre making his way towards the hotel. It was now the early hours of the morning.

Once or twice, he stopped to look around. He just wanted to make sure he wasn't being followed. Nothing seemed out of the ordinary, but he just had a feeling.

"Probably nothing," he muttered under his breath.

The girls and Titania were up bright and early the next morning making their way towards the breakfast room. They passed the reception desk; the large Troll who had stared at Rosie on arrival was there again. Rosie sensed him watching her closely as they walked by, making her feel uncomfortable. Thumblerock was sat in the dining room waiting for them, Rosie jumped on a seat next to him with his help.

"I'm not keen on the Troll behind reception – he keeps staring at me," she said.

"I've noticed," said Thumblerock.

"I don't want to make a fuss," she said.

"It's a good hotel, Rosie. Customers want to be treated with respect."

Breakfast consisted of lots of fruit, some pastries and breads, some cooked fish and eggs. Celaeno collected a selection for Rosie, as the display tables were just too high for her.

"Here you are," she said. "I've got you a bowl of assorted fruit, some bread and poached eggs."

"Thanks," said Rosie. "Is there any toast?"

"Er, not sure what that is, Rosie?"

"Well, you see bread like this, at home we cut it into slices, then we burn it slightly on both sides, then put butter and marmalade on it or jam." Celaeno was laughing hard, almost to the point of tears.

"Remind me not to come and visit," she said, in between giggles. Rosie started laughing, too.

"I guess it does sound a bit odd when I come to think about it."

"I've got the tickets for this evening's performance," said Titania.

"Wicked," said Rosie. Celaeno almost choked on her banana fruit.

"How can you use a word like that to express happiness?" asked Celaeno. "Your world is so strange."

"Well, I guess it just means it's so bad it's going to be really good." Celaeno shook her head, grinning.

"I'll try and use it at school to see my friends' reactions. I expect I'll be really popular with all these new words I'm learning from my Earth friend."

Thumblerock stood up and said, "Just some business to attend to. I'll meet you in the lobby when you've finished breakfast." Thumblerock walked back out into reception, it seemed quiet, and approached the Troll behind the counter.

"Could I see the manager, please?" The Troll seemed startled.

"Oh, I must apologise, he hasn't arrived yet. Is there something I can help you with?"

"Well, it's a little sensitive. Could we go into the office?"

"Oh yes, of course, sir, please come through."

Thumblerock followed him through a door into a small office behind reception. The office was empty. He closed the door behind him and stood in front of it.

"What's your name?" he enquired of the Troll.

"I'm Pleione," he said, now starting to look a little uncomfortable. Thumblerock was a large Troll, quite imposing and his attitude towards Pleione was making him nervous.

"I haven't seen you here before?" said Thumblerock.

"No, sir, I've not been working here long. What is it I can help you with?"

"You seem to be taking a keen interest in my companion from Earth. Why is that?"

Pleione's facial expression suddenly changed to one of defiance. "I don't often see visitors from other planets; I was merely inquisitive."

"Well now, there's your first lie," said Thumblerock. "Working in one of the best hotels in Sculptor, I expect you see off-world visitors on a daily basis. I'll ask you once again, what is your interest in her?" Thumblerock took a sudden step nearer to Pleione and grabbed the clothing around his neck.

"Who are you to assault me in this way?" Pleione squeaked.

"Let's just say I'm here on Council business," said Thumblerock.

The colour drained from Pleione's face. He stuttered, "I-I was just asked to-to watch you all and...report back."

"So," said Thumblerock, "it was you following me last night, wasn't it?" He squeezed the clothing around the Troll's neck a little tighter.

"Yes, yes. Please don't hurt me," he said, squirming.

"I won't, you miserable worm," said Thumblerock. "As long as you tell me who wants us watched?"

"I can't, they'll kill me," whimpered Pleione.

"Oh really," said Thumblerock. "And I won't?"

"Please, please, you don't understand," squealed Pleione.

Thumblerock hurled him against the wall with a loud crash. He drew a weapon from his pocket and held it to Pleione's head. "Do you know what this is?" Pleione shrieked. "Oh, you do. Good, then you will know the first time I use it. The pain is so intense you will tell me anything I want to know. The best outcome for you is to tell me now. Who do you report to?"

Pleione started to whimper again. "I only know the address; I never see anyone. I just hear a voice behind a door, and I pass on any information. That's all I know."

"Write the address down for me quickly?" said Thumblerock.

Sitting down at the small desk, Pleione scribbled down the address and passed it to him.

As Thumblerock was stood behind him, he moved a dial on his weapon, pressed it into the Troll's neck and squeezed the trigger. It made popping noise; Pleione shrieked.

"I haven't killed you yet," said Thumblerock. "You are now tagged. We know where you are now, and everyone you talk to, so I suggest you go and hide. It may just save your life, especially from your friends."

Thumblerock picked up the piece of paper and left the office. Pleione sat there shaking and rubbing the back of his neck. In the reception area, a few guests were stood waiting for some service.

"The receptionist won't be long," said Thumblerock. "He's just feeling a little unwell."

They looked at him a little confused. Just then, Titania came out of the dining room with the girls.

"Are we ready to go and meet the Council, Rosie?" asked Thumblerock.

"I am," she said, a little reluctantly, trying to conceal her nervousness.

Smiling, Thumblerock said, "Okay let's go, my brave little Earth friend."

Titania and Celaeno gave her a hug. "We'll see you later. Good luck," said Titania.

"I'll give 'em hell," said Rosie, and smiled.

Celaeno burst out laughing again as they separated. "You do that!" she shouted after her.

Thumblerock took her small hand as they left the escalator and walked across the plaza towards the portals.

"What do they really want of me?" she asked. Thumblerock stopped and knelt in front of her.

"They want to explain to you properly why you are here and how important you are in the whole contact process between our worlds. They also need to protect all the civilisations we share our galaxy with. Don't worry about it – you'll be fine."

Rosie was uncertain about the meaning of "protecting all the other civilisations". *From whom, us?* she thought. They continued to the portal and entered one of the booths.

"You have your motivator?"

"Yes, Rocky, it's in my hand."

Grasping her other hand, Thumblerock said, "Council Chambers." After which, they disappeared in a flash.

Rosie opened her eyes once she felt the ground beneath her feet again. They stepped out of the booth into an enormous entrance hall. The walls were made from the frosted white crystal. Waves of magical colours swept around the walls emanating a real sense of power. High above, a three-dimensional model of their part of the universe was rotating in the simulated blackness of space. She could see the fragile streams connecting worlds across vast distances. There was the Earth, far out on Orion's Spur, its wavering stream floating in the void.

Thumblerock led her across to a seating area and lifted her onto a comfortable red leather chair. A few other Trolls were also sat around in anticipation, obviously waiting for appointments.

"I just need to go and tell them we're here; I'll only be a few moments." He strode across towards a line of glass desks that encircled half of the hall. Each one was occupied by an attendant.

A female Troll occupying one desk gestured for him to sit in one of the seats in front of her. Rosie watched as Thumblerock started talking with her, but it was too far away to hear.

"I have an appointment to see the Secretary," he said.

"Hello, Rocky," said the girl. "It's good to see you again. I see you have a visitor with you?"

"I do," he replied. "My apologies, Maia. I didn't recognise you. I'm a little distracted today. How are you?"

"I'm well, thank you for asking."

"I wonder if you could do me a favour. My visitor is called Rosie. She's from Earth. Could you keep an eye on her whilst I'm with the Secretary?"

"Of course," she said. "It will be my pleasure to meet an earthling. I have a break shortly, should I take her for a tour of the building?"

"That's very gracious of you. I'm not really comfortable leaving her here; it's a bit of a foreboding place for a youngster."

"It's no trouble really," she said. "I'll call you as soon as the Secretary is available to see you."

Thumblerock returned to Rosie and sat down next to her. "Do you see the girl I was talking with? She's called Maia."

"I do," said Rosie.

"When I go in for my meeting, she has offered to show you around the building."

"Cool," said Rosie. "It looks amazing."

"Wait till you see the rest of it," he said. "This building has been here for about five hundred years. It was built to celebrate the power of the motivator crystal. Every use of the crystal is controlled through here, be it on-world or off-world travel. It's the focus of our modern existence."

A short time later, Maia approached them from across the hall. "She will see you now, Rocky."

"Thank you, Maia. May I introduce Rosie from Earth? It's her first time on our planet. She's been spending a few days with us on the farm before she returns to her home world."

"Hello, Rosie, I'm honoured to meet you."

"Hello, Maia. Gosh, you're pretty." Rosie was quite shocked by the female Troll's appearance close up. Black curly hair down to her shoulders and streaked with shining silver. A face with sharp features and bright glowing tangerine eyes, Rosie hadn't seen anyone like her since she'd been on Damianos.

Maia blushed and laughed a little; she could see Rosie studying her.

"I love your hair, and you have tangerine eyes. Are they natural?"

"Yes they are. I come from a land on the other side of the planet. Do you not have facial and colour differences in the people of Earth?"

"Yes, of course we do," said Rosie. "I should have thought. I'm sorry if I embarrassed you."

"I'm flattered that you think I'm pretty. I love your directness – it's an unusual trait on Damianos. You're also a beautiful girl; your hair is so long. I love it."

Thumblerock, a little impatient, broke into their conversation. "Maia is going to take you on a tour of the building. I must go."

"Come with me," said Maia. She helped her down from the chair. "Once we've completed the tour, Rocky, I'll bring Rosie through to the chamber lounge. It's a little more comfortable to wait for you there."

"That's good of you, Maia." He smiled at Rosie, turned and strode towards some imposing doors behind the glass desks. A Troll in uniform opened the door for him, and he disappeared through.

After navigating several corridors that he knew well, Thumblerock arrived at a door showing "General Secretary" on a gold plaque. He knocked, then went straight in without waiting for an answer.

An elderly female Troll was sat behind a desk. She struggled to her feet as Thumblerock approached. He thought that she looked tired and drawn.

"Madam Secretary, it's good to see you, it's been a while."

"It has, Rocky. I sense you bring me troublesome news. Why else would you request a private meeting?"

"I can only apologise for the urgency. My one wish is for peace and tranquillity."

She laughed. "So do we all."

Thumblerock took a seat, and the Secretary poured some water for him into a clear blue crystal glass. "How's your ward from Earth?" she asked.

"A quite remarkable, intelligent and sensible human being," replied Thumblerock.

"I've heard of her exploits in the village of Harlsey."

"Yes, Madam Secretary, that's only the beginning of her story. Her natural curiosity has uncovered an extremely troubling and deceitful plot, which may even extend to the Council itself. That's why I requested this meeting with you alone."

"Please go on," she said, and leaned back in her seat in anticipation. He started to talk.

"Three days ago, Rosie was on the beach at Lake Veyatie near our farm. She noticed three sets of boot prints in the sand heading along the shore. Two Trolls and one human. Before you ask me, Rosie brought her Earth dog with her, who confirmed the scent as human. Quizzical, a horse who lives with us, whom I hold in high esteem, also confirmed the unusual boot print. The following morning, myself, my neighbour Atlas, Hattie the Earth dog and Quizzical retraced Rosie's steps from the previous day. We followed the tracks towards a boat jetty, which were inconclusive following some overnight rain. We crossed the lake to the opposite jetty as we could see a boat moored there. With the Earth dog's help, we picked up the scent and followed it all the way up to the path separation in the foothills. One route led to the old portal at Mount Ahuna, and the other to the west. I established that they were heading for Mount Ahuna. As they'd had at least two days start on us, I decided to return and report the evidence I have so far to the Council."

Raising her hand, the Secretary said, "I appreciate your concern, but all of this so-called evidence is based purely on an Earth girl and her dog."

Thumblerock put his hand in his pocket, pulled out the drink can and handed it to her. "The dog found this discarded can in some undergrowth on our return to the lakeside."

The Secretary's posture changed; she studied the can with some concern.

"I have even further damning evidence to present to you which was given to me last night. My neighbour has kept a watch on the lakeside since I've been here in the city. We removed the boat they used to complicate their return should they reappear. Our actions made them change their plans and walk along the south side of the lake in the direction of Harlsey village. However, they were forced to bury a large heavy box they were carrying between them." Thumblerock took the sackcloth parcel from his other pocket and placed it on the desk in front of her.

The Secretary unwrapped the package and looked at the Earth weapon as well as two silver motivator boxes. She picked one up, and it immediately activated. Her shock and disbelief were plain to see. After composing herself, she looked at Thumblerock.

"Do you know of their whereabouts now?" she asked.

"We believe so. Atlas asked Hattie the Earth dog to carefully follow the Trolls to their destination. He remained behind, removed the remaining contents of the box and hid them in a safe place. He has repacked the box with rubble and sticks and buried it in its original location. I've asked him to continue to monitor the lakeside, but not to put himself at any further risk. I'm of course keen to return home once our business here is complete."

Sitting back in her chair, the Secretary considered all that Thumblerock had said. He remained silent, understanding that she needed to collect her thoughts. She then leaned forward and clasped her hands in front of her.

"First of all, let me congratulate you on the thoroughness of your report. It would seem we have a significant problem to deal with and potentially far-reaching consequences. I fully understand your insistence on this private meeting. Your ward, Rosie, and her dog may have accidently uncovered a plot of universal significance. I'm concerned that she may be in some danger."

"This was my concern as well, and it has already been borne out," said Thumblerock. "I tagged a male member of staff from the Asterope Inn. He was following me last night, and also taking a keen interest in Rosie's movements."

"Good," said the Secretary. "I'll have him monitored and picked up."

"How do you suggest we conclude the Council meeting with Rosie?" asked Thumblerock.

"We now have a complication in our plan to close the Earth gate," said the Secretary. "However, by returning Rosie to Earth and removing her motivator, this should reduce any potential threat to her. We can then focus on our new problem – how we close off further travel to and from Earth. We must find out who is responsible for this new technology. It could undermine security within the whole galactic travel network." The Secretary picked up one of the silver motivator boxes again and studied it.

"My concern," said Thumblerock, "is that we may have some highly placed individuals who do not agree with the Council policy of closing the Earth gate. They seem prepared to prevent it happening – by force if necessary."

"Rosie is also no longer the only traveller from Earth," said the Secretary. "How can we prevent common knowledge on that world of our existence? This is a dangerous situation for both our planets." She then added, "Thank you, Rocky, I intend to consult with my closest and most trusted colleagues. The meeting with Rosie must go ahead as planned; she must be returned home, and her motivator detained, for her sake as well as our own."

Chapter 9 Destiny of You

Rosie was enjoying her tour with Maia; however, this was tinged with a nervousness of the Council meeting to come. The building was enormous. They started with a tour of the library. It was filled with paintings, pictures, carvings, and animated scenes of events from history. Whilst they were there, various groups of school-aged youngsters were engaged in projects and studies.

"It's like a school field trip," she said. Maia looked a little confused with the terminology. "Maia," said Rosie, "can we go and just chat before my meeting with the Council? I'm not really in the mood for an extensive tour. I'd like to talk to you about your life in the city – it will take my mind off things."

"Of course, Rosie, come with me. We'll go to the chamber lounge where we can sit and have some refreshments."

They arrived at an area that was obviously not open to the general population. The carpet was now thicker, and the walls were elegantly decorated with marvellous views of the planet, as well as some spectacular off-world displays. Through some double doors, they entered a large lounge where comfortable seats and tables were spread around a semicircular glass wall overlooking a spectacular view of distant mountains.

"Is that a real view or is it projected?"

"No, it's real," said Maia. "We are at the back of the building on the edge of the city. The view looks over towards a mountain range we call the Tenzing Slopes. Let's go and sit near the windows."

A waiter came over, and Maia ordered iced juice and pastries.

"I hope you like them," she said.

"If it's cake, I'll be at the front of the queue," said Rosie.

Laughing, Maia replied, "I'm the same." Then she said, "So, what would you like to know?"

"Just tell me a little of your life in the city and how it all works. Where do you live? Do you have a partner? You know, just all the goss. It will distract me from thinking about the meeting."

Maia laughed out loud. "I think I know what you mean – I love that expression. I can see why Rocky and Alannah are so taken with you, Rosie. You show a zest for life in such a refreshing way. Well, to start with, I completed my education, and then I was lucky enough to be selected to join the team here at the General Council. It's a much sought-after role."

"I can see immediately why you were selected," said Rosie. "You're smart, you're beautiful and you look like you want more. I can see it in your eyes." Maia looked a little embarrassed.

"Well, I had no idea that humans were evolving into such sensitive and inquisitive creatures. The general impression taught is one of greed and violence from your race."

"It's easy to see how that impression has been created, Maia. I believe it reflects more about our system than its people. My friends and I, we all want a better life, one without conflict – and specifically to look after our planet, in the same way that you do. I think we're at the beginning of the process, though. Previous generations have ravaged its resources, and we are now starting to suffer the consequences."

"Don't assume this has always been a perfect world, Rosie. We have travelled through a similar time that you are in now. I've no doubt your planet will flourish once more."

"I do hope so," said Rosie.

"As for the other questions," continued Maia, "I live in accommodation provided by the Council. It's in a tall building by the lake on the east side of the city. No, I don't currently have a partner; and I'm happy about that. I need to focus on my career."

"I bet you get a lot of male attention?" asked Rosie. Maia laughed again.

"Yes, but we know how to deal with that, don't we!"

"What do you want to do, then? In your career, I mean."

"I've never told anyone else about this before except my parents, but I'd love the opportunity to work off-world as Thumblerock does."

"Well, why can't you? Don't tell me, it's a male dominated role."

Maia laughed out loud again. "Absolutely right. How perceptive of you."

"I can tell you, Maia, if I'd met you under the bridge on my home world for the first time, I wouldn't have gone through all the anguish of deciding whether to come here or not. No disrespect to Rocky; he's quite a scary figure."

Maia nodded and smiled. "Perhaps you can put in a good word for me with Thumblerock."

"Would that help?" asked Rosie.

"No, it was just a joke. Honestly, I don't want to burden you with my aspirations – you have enough to consider."

"Helping each other is where we all need to be," said Rosie.

Maia cleared a small tear from her eye with a tissue. "I'm going to miss you, and we've only just met."

"We'll meet again," said Rosie. "The next time it will be you standing in the tunnel on my world. I know it."

The waiter arrived with the drinks and pastries. They both pulled themselves together and giggled at him, as he looked a little confused with all the emotion around the table. He cleared his throat.

"I've been informed that the Council will see you in ten minutes, and Thumblerock will be here soon to accompany you."

"Thank you," said Maia. "We'll be ready."

A few minutes later, Thumblerock walked in and spotted them across the lounge. "Hello, you two. Have you enjoyed the tour, Rosie?"

"Yes," she replied, "and Maia has been wonderful company."

Maia smiled. "I've just been telling Rosie about my life in the city and here at the Council."

"Hmm," said Thumblerock. "She's been asking you lots of questions I suppose. She would make an excellent inquisitor. They come thick and fast."

They all laughed, and Thumblerock sat down with them and took a glass of juice and a pastry.

"Good choice," he said. "They will ask for us shortly, Rosie. Just answer any questions as simply as you can. I'm sure you'll have no problems."

"I can't wait," said Rosie.

Thumblerock looked at her a little confused, while Maia cracked up laughing.

"This has been going on for days now, Maia," he said. "I can't tell whether she's serious or joking."

The steward came across and said, "They will see you now."

They all stood up. Maia leant down and gave Rosie a little hug.

"It's been such a pleasure meeting you. I'll see you before you leave the building I hope."

"Thank you," said Rosie. "I've really enjoyed spending some time with you. See you later."

Maia watched them go. Thumblerock took Rosie's hand as he led her out of the lounge.

"Rosie," he said, "would you mind removing the necklace Atlas and Titania gave you? I just don't believe the Council need to know you have it." She looked at him curiously.

"Okay." She took it from around her neck and put it in her pocket.

A few corridors later, they arrived at huge oppressive-looking doors. They must have been ten metres high. A guard turned and grasped a large ring on one of the doors before swinging it open for them.

"Thank you," said Rosie, and Thumblerock nodded to him.

They entered a large room, a little like an amphitheatre. Walking down through a channel with seats above them on both sides, it seemed busy with chatter – although, as they approached the front, the noise subsided.

Thumblerock led Rosie to a large desk facing forwards with the seats behind her. Ahead and slightly above them was a long ornate wooden bench, curling around the raised staging area. Sat behind it were about a dozen male and female Trolls dressed in full official regalia. *It's just like a European Union Council meeting on Earth*, she thought.

A clerk on their right-hand side started banging his gavel to call attention. "Our special envoy Thumblerock of Damianos and his ward from Earth, Rosie," he called out.

Rosie took her seat with a little help from Thumblerock. A large male Troll sitting in the centre of the bench wearing flowing red and green robes and some peculiar-shaped glasses perched on the end of his nose stared directly at her.

"Welcome Rosie of Earth. I'm the Assistant Secretary. On behalf of us all here, I would like to welcome you to Damianos Central Council Chamber. We trust you have enjoyed your stay on our world."

Not waiting for a reply, he went on to explain the procedure.

"We have operated this system of introducing individuals to our world over many generations. I believe the last visitor from Earth was your great-grandfather Michael. Some of us here remember him well. We've welcomed other visitors from your ancestry stretching back in total for around two hundred cycles, or years in your terminology. We follow this process carefully through the generations so we can monitor the development of each planet harbouring intelligent life. The eventual outcome is usually the commencement of full contact once we believe a level of society and technical advancement has been achieved.

"Whilst you've only been here for a few days, we've already been informed of your heroic actions in saving one of our own children from a tragic accident. This is the first time an off-worlder in your position has been involved in such a magnificent act, and we will be forever in your debt. As a representative of the young people on Earth, you have made a significant impression on this Council and its people.

"However, it is with great regret that we have made the decision to suspend any further visitations from your world for a period of at least one hundred years. This will also require the return of your genetic motivator. I will explain the reasons behind our decision."

A stunned Rosie was about to speak when the Assistant Secretary saw this and held up his hand.

"You will have a right to reply in due course. Please be patient. As you know, each developed world that contains the motivator element embedded in its mantle is connected to all the other worlds by a fragile lightstream. A connection if you will. Over the millennia, we have developed a technology that allows us to monitor the health of a planet by the light spectrum projected within each stream. Should the light spectrum deteriorate within a stream, this would generally represent an environmental issue on a specific world. This can seriously affect the power flow around the universal network, and ultimately cause a draining effect within the whole system.

"I'm afraid we are here to inform you that this situation is developing on Earth. The effect on the light spectrum tells us that your planet is undergoing rapid change. Average temperature is increasing at quite an alarming rate. We can only surmise that this is being caused by environmental changes effected by the dominant species on your planet. Human beings. We hoped this situation could have been averted – but alas, the problem seems to be deteriorating rapidly.

"We are profoundly sorry that we have to deliver this news to you as the Earth's representative. Our only possible action is that the Earth must be cut off from the network to prevent further dissolution of the lightstream. This means there will be no further contact with the humans of Earth over this timescale. We can do this by removing your motivator once you have been returned to your home.

"To further simplify this explanation for you, the removal of your motivator from Earth will be like turning off an electrical circuit. The planetary link will remain;

however, there will be no flow of energy between our worlds' portals. This action will restore the balance around the galactic network."

Rosie stood with her head bowed.

"Do you understand what I have been saying to you?" asked the Assistant Secretary. "You are now free to reply."

Straightening up, Rosie summoned all her strength. This news was devastating – not just for her, but she was feeling ashamed for her whole planet.

"I'm fully aware of the issues we have on our planet – too much CO_2 being put into the atmosphere – we discuss it in school most days one way or another. The whole population of Earth is now looking for ways to resolve these problems. It's not that easy. You were lucky enough to discover the motivator crystal. I can see how that has influenced the development of your world.

"We haven't made that discovery as far as I'm aware. If we do, it will apparently send us all into chaos for generations. All I can say is we need help; we don't need to be cast aside to see if we manage the problem ourselves. Surely there's another way? How can you protect the network and help the Earth?" Rosie sat down, put her head in her hands and started to cry. "Why would you cast us aside so heartlessly?"

The Assistant Secretary rose again. "Thank you for your response, Rosie of Earth. However, the needs of developed worlds are our main consideration. I'm afraid the decision has already been made. We will continue to monitor the Earth's light spectrum. Should the situation improve at some future point within this time period, we will take steps to re-establish contact with a future member of your genetic family."

Rosie stared at them all as the Council members stood up and started to leave the chamber. They bowed their heads, not looking at her as they passed. Thumblerock tried to comfort her, but she was angry.

"You knew about this, didn't you, Rocky? This whole pretence of having a nice time here was to try and compensate for the big goodbye. I sensed from the first day that something was wrong." She directed another comment at the Council members as they were leaving the chamber. "Call yourselves an enlightened species? You're just acting like a corporation on Earth. You're totally selfish and ignorant of any consequences. You're all a disgrace."

Thumblerock tried to appease her. "Rosie, I won't deny it. I knew the Council would be taking these steps. All I can say is that all of us who have been involved with Earth are truly sorry. Regrettably, our voices aren't enough to influence the Council's decision. I'm afraid they are only looking at the bigger picture."

Rosie's tear-stained face stared up at the enormous Troll, her friend. She hugged him. "Rocky, I apologise. I'm not mad at you. I'm just extremely disappointed that a world which seems so advanced can make such a narrow-minded decision and wash their hands of us."

"I don't believe it's going to be that easy," said Thumblerock. "Those human footprints you discovered have opened up a real can of worms. Just removing your motivator may not be the solution they were hoping for."

Rosie, thinking about what he'd just said, looked at him a little confused. Then the penny dropped. "There's something you haven't told me?"

"Quite right," he said. "Not here, though. We'll talk later."

"Is that why you asked me to remove my necklace?"

"It might be. Let's get out of here."

They left the Council chamber and made their way to the entrance hall. Maia was sat in her seat and saw them approaching. She noticed the teary redness of Rosie's eyes.

"What's happened?" she directed her question to Thumblerock.

"Rosie must be returned home, and her motivator will be removed. They've decided to cut off Earth for a significant time due to the environmental issues on that planet. They are having a negative effect on the stellar transport network."

"Oh, that's awful. I don't know what to say."

"I know. I'm still trying to come to terms with it. It's been such a rollercoaster ride of emotions since I've been here. I've met such wonderful people; it's devastating."

Maia considered asking Rosie what a rollercoaster was but decided against it.

"We are taking Rosie to the theatre tonight to see the *History of the Motivator Crystal*. If you're free, Maia, would you like to join us?" asked Thumblerock.

"Oh please, Maia," said Rosie. "I want my last days on Damianos to be spent with the people who've become so important to me. Please come?"

"I'd love to," said Maia.

"Good," said Thumblerock. "We'll meet you there."

Chapter 10 A Night at the Opera

Rosie and Thumblerock returned to the hotel where he ordered lunch for both of them. Titania and Celaeno were out around the city. Atlas had given them a list of provisions he needed, and it was an opportunity for Celaeno to get hold of schooling items she couldn't get from home. They were due back shortly.

Rosie noticed the odd receptionist was no longer behind the counter.

"Must be his day off," said Thumblerock.

"Good," said Rosie. "I thought he was creepy."

A pleasant young waiter brought them some savouries and unusual small cakes for lunch. Rosie watched the people coming and going; she was in a bit of a daydream. She suddenly realised that Thumblerock was speaking to her.

"Sorry, Rocky, you said something?"

"I said I'm going to tell you a little of what I know because I believe some information about what is going on concerns your world. I don't want you to discuss this with anyone else whilst you are here as it could be dangerous for you and them. When you're back on Earth, this information may have some value for us both. Quite how the events will play out is still a mystery. You may yet have a part to play, my fine young friend. So don't be disheartened." Rosie looked at him keenly.

"The footprints on the beach and the drinks can," she said.

"Yes," said Thumblerock. "As well as some Earth weapons we found and four motivators which seem to work without any genetic recognition. This means anyone can use them! Technically, that's never been accomplished before. Each motivator would always need to be tied to its owner's genetic profile to enable travel. However, as far as the Council is concerned, we've only found two!"

"You found weapons as well?" The colour was draining from Rosie's cheeks.

"Yes, I'm afraid so," he said. "This is becoming a difficult situation." He thought for a moment, then continued, "What this means is that removing your motivator from Earth won't necessarily solve the problem. The energy flow within the lightstream will still be active if there are other unidentifiable motivators on Earth that can't be traced. The Council won't know this until you've been returned and I've removed your motivator from your planet. No, this is not the end, Rosie; I believe it's just the beginning."

"Do you think they will be using the portal in the tunnel near Grandma's house or could there be others on Earth?" she asked.

"I just don't know, Rosie. Different portal locations should have shown up in the travel records. You can bet the scientists are rushing around now following my report to the Secretary. My only reluctance is dragging you deeper into this mystery and risking your safety."

"As long as it keeps the window open for me, Rocky, I'll do anything you ask. I can't bear to think that I may not see any of you ever again."

"I know you will. That's why I didn't want you to show the Council your Star of Alcyone. I'll be able to use it to contact you even though you won't have your motivator, should I travel to Earth at a future date. When I arrive, it will link with my motivator and vibrate. I just need to pair them before we leave."

"You have other communications devices, Rocky; I've seen them. Can you use those to call me when you arrive?"

"I could, but as you've probably noticed, we don't use them much, especially in my profession. Calls can easily be intercepted. What I suggest is that when your necklace vibrates, we'll arrange to meet the following day at the same time. Let's discuss this in more detail whilst we are travelling to Earth tomorrow."

Just then, Titania and Celaeno came in carrying bags.

"Can I order you some lunch?" asked Thumblerock.

"Yes please," answered Celaeno. "I'm hungry."

Thumblerock got up to leave the table and whispered in Rosie's ear, "Not a word about our discussion," and patted her shoulder.

"How was your meeting with the Council, Rosie?" asked Titania.

"It wasn't pleasant," she said. "I've been informed that they are going to close the Earth gate. This is due to Earth's environmental issues and the impact on the transport network."

"Oh, Rosie, that's awful," said Titania. "Thumblerock, can't you help? Surely the Council will listen to you?" she asked when he returned to the table.

"I'm afraid not. I've told them how I feel about it and the potential of the human race. They're only interested in preserving the status quo. They didn't get off lightly, though. Rosie gave them a good telling off. I was proud of her; they deserved it."

"On a positive note," said Rosie, "the building was beautiful, and I met Maia. She's coming with us tonight."

"Is she a colleague of Rocky's?" asked Celaeno.

"She is, and she was lovely to me, showing me around whilst Rocky was busy."

"At least it's over with. We didn't expect there would be a positive outcome about Earth. We've all heard the whispers," said Celaeno.

That afternoon, Thumblerock left them to their own devices; he needed to be elsewhere. "I'll be back later. Have a pleasant afternoon. We leave for the theatre at five and a carriage is booked. See you later." With that, he left the hotel.

"Rosie, you need something to wear tonight," said Celaeno. "You can't go in your jeans and boots. Where shall we take her, Titania?"

"Well, let's go out and see. Perhaps reception can direct us; after all, they get many off-world visitors here." So off they went. Rosie was excited at the prospect of having a new outfit from Damianos.

They discussed a few options with a pleasant female receptionist and set off. It was still cold; a piercing wind whistled across the plaza. They walked for a few minutes, then entered a set of large frosted crystal doors into a shopping mall. All the shop fronts sported visual displays of goods they were selling. There didn't seem to be any real items on show, just a shop attendant sat or stood behind a console.

"Your shops are so different to ours," said Rosie. "We have actual goods filling all the shops on shelves and racks. You just look through items and choose what you want. Where do they keep all their stock?"

Celaeno looked at her a little confused. "Oh, they don't keep any stock. That would be wasteful. If you need something, you select it on a console from a particular shop and they make it for you on the premises."

"Wow," said Rosie. "That's amazing – what a simple idea. We don't have anything like that level of technology. It would completely transform our planet, as we move goods all over our world. I guess that's why it's in such a mess."

"Here we are," said Titania. "Let's try this shop."

They entered a pleasant little store with consoles scattered uniformly across the floor space. Behind them against the walls were glass cabinets with mannequins inside. The clothing was being made by machines and the mannequins were being dressed by robot arms all at the same time. Customers were standing in front of each cabinet watching the progress – it was mesmerising. Other customers were standing looking at consoles, flipping electronic pages backwards and forwards and giving verbal instructions.

A shop assistant approached them; it wasn't a Troll, though. It was a much smaller being of a similar size to Rosie, although squatter and broader, with a more complex face and pale with big eyes, a small mouth, no nose that she could see and no hair. Rosie was a little shocked by its appearance.

"Can I help you with a selection?"

Titania stepped in. "Greetings to you. We would appreciate some assistance in selecting an outfit suitable for a visit to the theatre for our off-world friend here," she said, indicating to Rosie.

"An earthling, if I'm not mistaken. This is such an honour; I've never met an earthling before."

"Hello," said Rosie. She extended her hand. "Are you an off-worlder, too?"

The creature looked at her hand a little confused, then produced its own limb from under a flowing robe and touched Rosie's hand. "I hope I greeted you correctly?" it said.

"Close enough," said Rosie, now smiling.

"I'm from a world called Gliese. It's a warm world. I apologise if my appearance shocked you. I scare myself sometimes." Rosie laughed out loud. "Ah, a refined sense of humour," said the creature. "We'll get on well. These Trolls can sometimes be hard work. I like humans already. Perhaps I should open a shop on Earth?"

"I think you should," said Rosie. "You'll go down a storm. What should I call you?"

"Just Gliese. We don't have individual names."

"Well, I'm pleased to meet you, Gliese. I'm Rosie."

"A trip to the theatre. Well, let's see."

Gliese produced a handheld machine and proceeded to scan Rosie from head to toe. A cabinet activated at the same time, and a three-dimensional image of Rosie was created inside. It was a little nondescript to save embarrassment; however, the dimensions were perfect, as was Rosie's face.

"Now, let me show you some examples of the latest fashion." Costumes started to appear on the mannequin for Rosie to look at. "Just sweep from right to left in front of the cabinet, and a different costume will be displayed. Let me know when you find something you like. Or you could have a go at designing your own?"

Celaeno and Titania joined in to help Rosie, so the attendant retreated to give them space. After they had suggested a few ideas, the cabinet immediately reacted by incorporating the suggestions.

"Wow," said Rosie. "What a cool way to shop." Both Titania and Celaeno were amazed at how quickly Rosie had adapted to the technology. She began to design her costume.

"Why don't you base it on a design from your world?" said Celaeno. "We'd love to see it."

"I can try," said Rosie. She manipulated the console and eventually settled on an example that looked like an Indian dress from Earth. A royal blue long-sleeved top with a split in the collar and edged with a silver trim. It was tight fitting on top, but flowed down like a dress. This was accompanied with leggings of lighter blue decorated with blocks of silver and white, a silver shawl and white shoes with a modest heel.

"Rosie, that's amazing," said Celaeno. "I've never seen such a dress design. Are they popular on Earth?"

"Yes, I would say so. It's not something I would normally wear, but I've always loved Indian clothing."

Gliese came over and admired the creation. "How exquisite. I'll certainly be adding that design to my catalogue, with your permission?" she said. "Would you come and work with me? I need to see more human clothing ideas?"

"I'd love to," said Rosie. "Unfortunately I have to return home soon."

"What a shame," said Gliese, a little disappointed.

"We'll have that, then," said Titania.

Gliese bowed, pressed a few buttons on the console, and the cabinet started to generate the clothing design. Only a few minutes later, the shop assistant was packing the clothing into a box with tissue paper.

"Could you send it to the Asterope Inn?" asked Titania.

"Of course," said Gliese. "It will be waiting for you at reception."

"Please charge it to the General Council's account?"

"Of course, madam." Gliese extended a limb towards Rosie, and she touched it again. "Thank you for choosing my store; you have made my day. My family will be most interested to hear all about my meeting with an enchanting earthling." Rosie waved at Gliese as they left the shop.

"Some refreshments I think," said Titania. They crossed the shopping mall heading for a food court bustling with Trolls of all ages. They took a table with a good view so Rosie could watch as Trolls wandered about their business.

Rosie asked, "Was Gliese male or female, I couldn't decide?"

"No, they're hermaphrodites," replied Celaeno.

"Oh," said Rosie. "I guess that makes sense and why I couldn't work it out."

"They are a kind and gentle race," said Celaeno. "They typically run shops or provide services; they have endless patience."

"I can tell," said Rosie. "I liked him, or her." Celaeno laughed out loud.

"You're so funny. Do you do it on purpose?"

"I might do. I'm not really sure," she said.

They finished their drinks, and then wandered around the mall. Titania left the girls to themselves. Celaeno showed Rosie where all the younger Trolls would collect with friends and the shops or entertainment venues they would visit. It was surprisingly similar to how teenagers would behave on Earth. They wanted to be together, to meet new boys or girls, and enjoy time away from parents or school. Just to hang out, as Rosie suggested to Celaeno, who was definitely going to use that phrase again.

They eventually made their way back to the hotel and met up with Thumblerock and Titania having afternoon drinks in the hotel lounge.

"We need to go and get ready shortly," said Titania.

"Yes, yes, we need to board the carriage by five," said Thumblerock. "We can have a meal at the theatre before the performance." The girls were obviously excited.

"Why don't you two go to the room and shower?" said Titania. "I'll be up shortly to help with your costumes."

So off they went giggling and laughing towards the room.

"You have a lot on your mind, Rocky?" asked Titania.

"I do," he said. "I'd like to tell you, but I can't. The events of the last few days have serious implications for both Rosie's planet and ours. I need to get her home tomorrow."

"To Earth, you mean?"

"Yes, for now I'd feel happier if she were back home. She'll be much more anonymous there. Here, she is vulnerable."

"I didn't realise she was in any danger. I've let them wander around the city today alone. I never thought."

"It was taken care of, Titania, don't worry. A friend of mine kept a close eye on them all afternoon, so they were safe. I would never put them at risk or have passed that responsibility on to you."

"Rocky, you need to go and get some rest. You look tired out. We don't need to board the carriage until five. Wait until you see Rosie's costume. She designed it herself; she's a talented girl – there's no doubt."

"Yes, I agree, one of the finest youngsters I've brought here. They just get smarter and more capable with every generation, and they need to in this universe. Politics, governments, worlds, disagreements, negotiations – it's so complex," said Thumblerock.

"Have you considered giving it all up, Rocky?"

"I have, and Alannah is also of the same mind. It's such a strain on her, managing the farm in my absence and worrying if I'm going to return from each trip."

"We'd all like to see you home for good, Rocky. I can't imagine how she copes. We'll always be there for her – you know that."

"I know. You're good friends, all of you. Come on, let's move."

The girls all competed for space in the hotel bathroom as they prepared for their evening out. Rosie giggled as she considered how similar the process was regardless of which world you were on. Celaeno wore a fashionable dress and a jacket of sparkles. Her mother, a sophisticated long gown and long black coat to keep out the chill.

They arrived a little late in the hotel lobby. Thumblerock was sitting at a lounge table waiting. He was a little frustrated at their timekeeping as well as being hungry. He'd only eaten a small pastry in the Council lounge, so he was looking forward to some good food at the theatre. They travelled up the escalator where a carriage was waiting for them.

Rosie was happy and excited; her new outfit was a perfect fit. Thumblerock was impressed. He took some images of them all together on a handheld unit he produced from his pocket.

"I'll send them on to Alannah. She'll be amazed at your dress design skills, Rosie."

The girls boarded the beautiful carriage. Once again, it reflected a stagecoach from the Wild West era on Earth. Chintzy curtains, red and green velour seats, and the hotel motif and colour scheme displayed in gold lettering on the doors. Another surprise was two fabulous horses rigged up and ready to pull the carriage – no motivator for this trip. Thumblerock was last to board after a quick word with the horses.

"Well, this is a treat," he said as he climbed in.

"You've arranged all this, haven't you?" asked Rosie. He smiled but said nothing. "Rocky," she began, "I can't help but notice the similarity to Earth's history. This carriage looks like it's straight from the eighteenth-century period of the Wild West on Earth?"

"You're right about that. Remember, we've been visiting your planet for many centuries. We take ideas from many worlds if they can add to our cultural diversity. This period from your world has a particular fascination for us."

"It's lovely," said Rosie. "I'm so impressed by the detail."

The horses clopped along the impressive roadways; stunning architecture drifted by all lit up by artificial lights of dazzling colours. The background lighting concealed within the road allowed the horses to safely follow their route. It was early evening, so not too many Trolls around. A few brave souls were scurrying between buildings, trying to keep out of the wind. Inside the carriage was pleasantly warm with the soft hum of background music.

"Have you seen this performance before?" asked Rosie. They all shook their heads.

"It's one of those historical dramas that we all should see but is generally only seen by visitors," said Titania.

"I know what you mean," said Rosie. "I hope you won't be bored by it."

"Quite the contrary," said Thumblerock. "We will all hopefully learn something. I'm actually looking forward to it."

When they arrived at the theatre, the horses pulled up in an area set aside for carriages. An usher opened the door and helped all the ladies out of the carriage. They stepped onto a royal blue carpet, which led up a set of broad stairs to the entrance doors.

As they approached, the doors swung open automatically allowing them to walk through into a foyer. It was just as you would expect a theatre to be decorated, with wood panelling and large crystal chandeliers, and there were advertisements of current and future shows showing as 3D projections in the space above the ticket desks.

"Awesome," said Rosie.

Thumblerock approached a desk and was directed by another usher towards their seats, through another set of double doors and into the performance hall itself. All around were raised circular booths quite some distance above ground level. He led them to a position almost central in the theatre, with the floor sloping far away towards the stage. It must have been at least a hundred metres away.

"Everyone stand inside this circle." The usher pressed a button on the floor with his boot. The circular platform they were standing on began to rise. As it rose with them stood on it, a semicircular bench seat appeared out of the floor. Thumblerock ushered them onto the seats. Once all were sat down, a semicircular table began to rise in front of them. Rosie was amazed. Thumblerock gave her a booster cushion so she could sit at the same level as the others. She could now lean on the table if she so wished.

The platform came to a halt ten metres from the ground. The view was amazing; it sloped away down towards the staging area.

"Is everyone hungry and in need of a drink, I know I am?" asked Thumblerock. He pressed some buttons on the table in front of him, and a selection of food and drink dispensers rose out of the table. He poured the girls some punch in iced crystal glasses. He and Titania helped themselves to something a little stronger.

The food was displayed in a buffet style, with an ornate semicircular plate for each of them to fit the table edge. A variety of dishes slowly rotated past them.

"I'm coming here again," said Rosie, to which they all laughed. "Where's Maia?" she then asked all of a sudden.

"She'll be along, Rosie. She's been sorting a few things for me," answered Thumblerock.

"I'm glad she's still coming; I want to see her again before I leave."

The theatre was quite busy. Rosie looked around at some of the tables nearby. Titania was correct: a lot of them were populated with off-worlders and their Troll chaperones. She could see several beings who were obviously not Trolls; it was hard not to stare. One or two of them waved at her doing the same thing.

There was a knock on the door behind them, and Maia appeared a little flushed.

"You look like you've been rushing," said Rosie.

"A little, I guess," she replied.

Rosie began to introduce her new friend to the others. Maia looked stunning. Her hair was raised up with silver clips and white feathers. She wore a slim black and silver patterned dress, which complemented the silver streaks in her hair, silver high-heeled shoes and a silver and black short imitation fur jacket. Her make-up followed the same colour scheme, silver and black eyeliner to accentuate those fabulous glowing orange eyes. Celaeno and Titania were agog.

"Well now, Rocky," said Titania, "you've never told us about your beautiful colleague."

"It's the selection process," said Thumblerock. "As you can see, we expect high standards." They all laughed; Maia looked a little embarrassed.

"Rocky," said Rosie, "on Earth, if you made a comment like that, you'd be charged with sexism. It's all the rage now."

"Well, I'm glad we're not there," he said. "Maia is a capable and beautiful colleague; she's a credit to our race. I expect my role is at serious risk from this younger generation, and I welcome it."

"And that's ageist," said Rosie, and they all howled with laughter.

"A drink, Maia?" asked Thumblerock.

They settled into their seats, Rosie in the middle with Celaeno on one side and Maia on the other. Thumblerock and Titania sat together so they could make use of the alcohol dispenser. It was turning into a special evening. Lots of chatter, laughter and a few tears from Rosie, and that was all before the performance had begun.

The theatre darkened. Ahead and above a three-dimensional representation of Damianos appeared spinning in the void all alone. Slowly the planet approached, until a small boat was shown bobbing on the sea. A small sail billowed in the wind, and a family of Trolls huddled in the rear fighting the weather. It wasn't a movie as at home – it looked so real. The people in the boat were real actors, as though suspended in mid-air.

With the roar of the sea, the spray sheeted over the boat's bow as it plunged into the trough of the wave before hurtling out over the next crest. Land was approaching through the mist; the characters were shouting and gesticulating to each other. They all stared at the new land coming into view.

The scene then changed. A small village was growing along a river estuary before their eyes. Lots of hammering on new buildings, commerce, ships sailing in and out. Rosie could see real characters moving around every building, on every ship, riding horses, pulling carts – it was magical. It took her breath away, so vivid were the images.

Smoke from chimneys, factories with workers walking towards them to toil, and even what looked like coal miners with black faces and white eyes appearing from mine entrances. Animals being used and whipped, working in fields, even being slaughtered for food. Rosie gasped, and Maia squeezed her hand. It was brutal, and obviously meant to be.

The scene changed again. Some Trolls were working at one of the Poles in some scientific expedition. A meteor was seen hurtling towards the planet, and there was a large crater. Down they went investigating. A sudden glow emanated from the crater; something deep down in the mantle was exposed. Suddenly, in the evening darkness, a rainbow of colours sprang from the crater and radiated into the night sky. Scientists were now in a lab working with small dices of white crystal.

Once the lights came up, the scene dissipated. Rumbles of conversations grew around the theatre. Rosie turned her head towards them all. Quite exhausted by the tension within the performance, tears were still running down her little human face. The first part of the story took over an hour, but it only seemed like minutes, as each vision was so powerful and enthralling.

Maia produced a tissue and dabbed Rosie's face gently to not spoil her make-up.

"There'll be a short break," said Thumblerock. "Go and stretch your legs if you need to."

As well as Rosie, the others were also moved by the performance.

"Good idea," said Titania.

All the girls left the booth, leaving Thumblerock to replenish his drink and settle back into his seat with his feet up.

His mind had now switched to the consideration of Rosie's return to Earth. They would leave the city shortly after breakfast tomorrow and arrive at the farm late morning before preparing for their return trip to Earth. He planned to leave the farm for the portal at dusk. After a stopover of eight hours at the Earth Way Station, they would be on Earth by the following afternoon. Their motivators would coordinate their exact arrival time on Earth to match their leaving time a few days before.

That was the plan anyway. The Council were now investigating the evidence he'd presented and organising for the rogue Trolls to be picked up – assuming they were still in the vicinity. Atlas reported no further activity around the lake. Once he'd delivered Rosie home safely, his next port of call was the so-called abandoned portal at Mount Ahuna. He would use one of the unusual motivators he had kept hold of, without the Council's knowledge. He was sure they could unlock more of the mystery. He wondered how far this deception had spread within the Council members. Rosie then returned first by herself.

Surprised, Thumblerock asked, "Where are the others?"

"Oh, all chatting in the foyer to people Maia knows. I told them I was going to keep you company."

Thumblerock laughed. "You're a thoughtful soul, Rosie. It's unusual on our world; most Trolls just wouldn't make the effort. It may all seem so perfect to you here, but there's a lot of disenchantment on this world. Individuals don't care as much anymore – like the spark has gone out of them. Don't get me wrong, it's not something you could easily discover as a visitor. What I mean is, we have a good life, new discoveries are limited however, and people can get a little complacent.

"Your world, on the other hand, is still at the beginning of major developments. Full of both excitement and fear. This makes people do strange and ugly things at times. Out of the chaos your planet is now facing, order could come. It will be up to you and young people like you to influence the direction of progress on your world."

"Crikey," said Rosie. "I wish I'd stayed in the foyer with the others." Thumblerock looked at her strangely for a second, then rolled around laughing, so surprised at the retort.

"Your grandfather used to have me in stitches as well. It's been a long time since I've laughed like this."

The others filed back in a little concerned at the tears on Thumblerock's face. They looked at Rosie.

"What's happened?"

Thumblerock answered, "Apologies, it's just Rosie being Rosie – she was just trying to cheer me up."

They all took their seats as the theatre darkened once more.

Flames erupted in villages and towns, weapons of fierce colour fired, and people ran screaming. Ships battled on the oceans; animals lay dead and dying. This plague of destruction seemed to sweep the whole planet. The spinning world was dark and poisoned.

Negotiations started, settlements were rebuilt, factories were formed across the planet. They produced small silver boxes with an opaque crystal inside. Each mature Troll was gifted one, carefully configured by scientists to limit the power for peaceful purposes. Farms and communities began developing, harnesses were removed from animals, and fences and barriers were torn down. Over time, larger animals began conversing in limited ways with Trolls. As generations passed, this ability began to cascade down to the smaller animals and birds.

It showed how the motivator crystal was crucial in the mental development of the Trolls. From the dominant species on the planet to the protectors of the environment and all its lifeforms. National governments disappeared, and a ruling Council was created to oversee the further development of the whole society on Damianos. A period of calm and prosperity was created.

The focus of the story now moved off-world, where astronauts above the planet occupied space stations experimenting with the new technology. Slowly, a map of lightstreams like invisible cords radiated out across the universe and linked up with other planets. The first Troll travelled and appeared on another world.

Each planet in turn was visited. Different races stood together with Trolls, and commerce flowed backwards and forwards. It gave the impression of partnerships between races across the cosmos. The Trolls seemed to sit at the centre of their universe; peace and harmony was being extended to all.

Less technologically advanced worlds were visited, and plans were put in place to monitor a society's development through their children. The eventual outcome being their eventual invitation to join the universal community.

The last vision began to fade, and the theatre lights were coming back on. Around the theatre, applause was rippling around the auditorium. Rosie could see the other off-worlders laughing, clapping and congratulating their hosts. It all seemed a little too perfect. She looked at Thumblerock and smiled, and he smiled back at her. She knew that he understood how she was feeling.

Titania and Celaeno were enthusiastic and buoyant about their world's achievements. They smiled with pride at the end of the performance. Rosie beamed and congratulated them for their planet's extraordinary development path. She noticed that Maia was not quite so moved.

Maia looked at Rosie and winked, and then whispered in her ear on their way out, "Nothing like a good piece of propaganda to show off all our achievements."

Rosie grinned at her. She wasn't surprised at her cool reaction; after all, Thumblerock and Maia were in the front line of galactic politics. Something the general population could never hope to understand.

They made their way out of the theatre and down the steps to the waiting carriage. Titania and Celaeno boarded, which left Thumblerock, Rosie and Maia standing a little awkwardly on the steps.

"Maia," said Rosie, "I'm feeling sad just now; this may be the last time we ever see each other."

"That may be true," she replied. "It's been a wonderful experience for me to meet and spend some time with you. I will never forget you, Rosie. You have been an inspiration to me in so many ways."

"Have you told Rocky that you would like his job?" asked Rosie.

Maia instantly flushed with embarrassment; she was completely caught off guard.

Thumblerock let out a raucous laugh, then added, "I can't think of a better candidate," and smiled at Maia. "Should I choose to step down of course."

Maia knelt and swept Rosie up in her arms. "Be happy and excel in everything you do, and of that I have no doubt." Tears rolled down Maia's face, spoiling her make-up. This time Rosie dabbed them off with a tissue from her pocket.

After helping Rosie into the carriage, Thumblerock shared a few private words with Maia before climbing in himself. Maia then walked over to the horses and spoke softly to them. They started to slowly pull the coach away, turning into the road to retrace their steps in the direction of the hotel. Rosie waved madly at the window and blew kisses towards Maia; in turn, she repeated the gesture, and then turned and walked away in the opposite direction.

Chapter 11 The Journey Home

Thumblerock gave them clear instructions to be up early and down for their last breakfast in the city. Each of them were rushing around taking turns in the bathroom and collecting their belongings. Of course, Thumblerock sat a little impatiently at the restaurant table, checking his timepiece and muttering under his breath.

Eventually, they came through the door into the restaurant. Titania, looking a little stressed, smiled apologetically at him. He smiled back and beckoned them to the table.

Breakfast was taken in quite high spirits. Rosie was eager to see Hattie, and Titania was happy to be going home. Only Celaeno was a bit fed up. She'd really enjoyed her time with her new Earth friend, but now it was all over. Worse than that, Rosie was also leaving the planet. She was feeling quite miserable.

Rosie tried to cheer her up, eventually getting a smile by saying, "I know it really sucks." Celaeno took out her little notebook and wrote this latest phrase in amongst the others.

"Thank you, Rosie, at least I can introduce all these new terms to my friends at school. All the parents won't have a clue what's going on – it's going to be so cool." They both laughed out loud.

Rosie took one last look back at the hotel before passing through the swing doors. Trying to commit as much to memory as she could, she'd already decided to write down her whole experience once back at home.

They crossed the chilly plaza heading for the portals to take them back to the farms. Rosie was reunited with her motivator. Thumblerock had been looking after it since they'd arrived in the city. As her cold fingers wrapped around it, she could feel the tingling sensation and smiled. *Was it all just a dream?*

She was slowly becoming used to portal travel. The initial nauseous feeling was now not such a problem. She kept her eyes shut, though, as the motivator hurled them towards their destination. They emerged from the old oak into the bright sunlight and followed the path down to the oculus for the carriage ride to the farms.

Once in the carriage, they either dozed or looked out of the windows in silence.

After a while, Thumblerock said, "No more than an hour and we'll be home." They all nodded and returned to their thoughts.

It was a dog bark that jolted Rosie out of her snooze. She could see Hattie at the end of the track sitting waiting for them. The carriage pulled up, and she jumped out. Hattie ran over excitedly, nuzzling her knees and enjoying the welcome home back rub. Thumblerock jumped down.

"We'll walk up to the farm from here and let these two get home to Atlas and Callisto," he said.

Titania and Celaeno climbed out of the carriage realising that this was possibly the last time they would ever see Rosie. It caught them by surprise.

"Oh, Rosie, it's been such a pleasure. You've brought such joy into our lives. We'll all miss you terribly." Celaeno was in tears as Titania hugged Rosie.

"I love you all," said Rosie. "My new family on Damianos, I won't forget you; and just maybe we'll meet again, who knows. Say goodbye to Atlas and Callisto for me. Tell

Callisto to stay away from the fish slide and think of a different career!"

"We will," said Celaeno, smiling. She gave Rosie a big hug, and then climbed back into the carriage in floods of tears. Titania followed and put her arm around her daughter as the carriage moved silently away.

"Come on, Rosie. Alannah is waiting for us. We must prepare for another journey," said Thumblerock.

Rosie grasped his hand as they walked up the winding track towards the farm. Hattie followed closely looking a little sad. She stopped to watch the carriage disappear around the corner.

"She knows," said Thumblerock, "in her own way."

"You must have done this quite a number of times, Rocky?"

"I have – it gets harder and harder every time."

A few minutes later, they walked into the farmyard. Alannah saw them coming and ran over excitedly to hug them both.

"Dear Hattie," she said, "she's been sitting up there waiting for you for at least two hours. She's such an innocent, and totally devoted to you, Rosie."

"I know. We all love her to bits. Do you mind if I take her for a walk? I want to tell her all about Sculptor and that we're going home today. She needs to prepare for it. I expect it will be a shock for her to revert to being just a dog on Earth! Maybe she'll understand some of it."

"Of course," said Thumblerock. "Take your time. There's no rush."

Rosie and Hattie walked across the yard and into the barn. Ceres and Quizzical were standing chewing hay from a circular rack surrounding one of the posts that supported the roof. The horses turned to look at them, nodded and blew through their nostrils with excitement.

"Hello, you two. Hattie and I are going for a short walk before we leave for home. We just wanted to come and say goodbye."

The two horses turned and approached them slowly. Quizzical gently pushed Rosie back towards the door with Ceres following.

"Oh," said Rosie, "you want to come for a walk, too?" Both horses whinnied and nodded.

So all four of them walked out into the farmyard and down the lane through the fields. Thumblerock and Alannah watched them leave through the kitchen window and then looked at each other.

"For a young Earth girl without the language skills we have, she's developed a strong bond with all the animals," said Alannah. They returned to their table and sat down, both having to cope with a sudden terrible feeling of sadness.

"This isn't the way it's supposed to be, Alannah. Something must be done."

"What can be done, Rocky? The Council has ruled."

On their walk, Rosie began to describe her visit to Sculptor as simply as she could. The hotel, the shops and the people she had met. The animals walked along in complete silence listening and nodding. After a while, Hattie ran ahead and started sniffing and rummaging around in the hedge. The horses stayed with her, one on each side matching Rosie's pace.

After walking all the way down to the edge of the lake, Rosie slipped off her boots and socks and paddled along the shore. As expected, Hattie charged into the water, followed by the horses. She watched them swimming and frolicking around chasing each other. Hattie occasionally barked and splashed with her front paws if one of the horses got to close. It looked like a game of tig.

She sat down on the beach and brushed the drying sand off her feet. After putting her socks and boots back on, Rosie stood up and shouted them.

"Come on, it's time to go." She felt a wave of sadness wash over her. Was this the last time she would be here? Rosie just didn't know. Realistically, she thought it probably would be, regardless of what Thumblerock had previously said. After all, how useful could a young almost teenage girl be in the complex world of universal politics?

The animals came out of the water and shook themselves all over Rosie.

"You're doing that on purpose." The horses vigorously nodded their heads up and down, and Hattie barked and chuntered. "Oh, so that's funny is it?" said Rosie, and the horses snorted. Hattie rolled around in the sand to dry off and stop the itching dampness with legs up in the air and grunting with pleasure.

They walked slowly back up the hill. It was a warm day, causing the horses to steam as the water evaporated from their coats.

"Hattie, listen to me. I need you to understand that we are leaving here today and travelling home. I don't expect you will ever see your new friends again. You need to say goodbye. Do you understand?"

She barked a few times and grumbled. The horses, obviously moved by Rosie's words, also became quite vocal.

When they reached the farmyard, a carriage was there waiting for them. Rocky had obviously walked up to the oculus to retrieve it.

After hugging the horses in turn, she watched them slowly walk back into the barn. There was a final look from Quizzical, who snorted before disappearing inside. Rosie and Hattie then went into the kitchen.

"I've made some food for both of you before you leave," said Alannah. At the sound of food, Hattie shot over to her bowl and got stuck in.

Rosie washed her hands in the kitchen sink and sat down at the table. A bowl of fish and vegetable broth sat steaming in front of her. Realising how hungry she was, she picked up a crust of bread and dipped it in.

"I'll really miss the taste of the food here, Alannah, it's so sweet and scrumptious. It just reminds me of Damianos itself."

"You have a task to complete before you leave," said Alannah.

"Do I?" asked Rosie.

"Yes, I've left a writing implement and some parchment in your bedroom. You need to write to your great-grandchild as Michael wrote for you."

"Oh, I'd quite forgotten. What shall I say? The Council made it quite clear that Earth was to be shut off for at least a hundred years and they're taking my motivator away."

"Just do as we have always done across the generations. Whether it's a further distant relative of the future no one knows; these are uncertain times."

Rosie finished her meal and trudged upstairs to complete what she thought an onerous task. On the dressing table was a roll of parchment and a beautiful pen just like an old-fashioned quill. *How quaint*, she thought. Although, as soon as she picked it up, that thought was quickly dispelled.

She started to write; the pen flowed almost without her putting any physical effort into it. Rosie realised that the pen was tapping directly into her thoughts. "It must have a motivator crystal inside it," she muttered. Feeling the gentle tingling through her fingers, it was as though the writing was not in her own hand.

Hello distant relative,

My name is Rosie and I'm a distant relative of yours. I came to this planet with Thumblerock in the year 2020 on Earth. I have seen such beautiful and magical things, and enjoyed the wonderful connection between all the animals and the Trolls of this world. My grandma's dog, Hattie, came with me; and unbelievably she can be understood by the Trolls. In fact, all the animals here can communicate in their own way with each other. It's all down to the motivator crystal, which has helped to create this society over many generations. If you are here, it must mean that the environmental issues on our planet have been solved. I hope the humans of your future have joined the universal community. Enjoy your time here, and don't go too near the fish slide in Harlsey. That's another story!

All my love, Rosie and Hattie.

Rosie put the pen down and read through the letter again. She pulled out Michael's letter and compared them. The script was written in the same hand. So here the pen does the writing. *I guess it makes sense*, she thought, *as some people's freehand is almost illegible*.

She rolled up the parchment and tied it with some yellow ribbon that Alannah had left for her. After placing it in the dressing table drawer along with Michael's, Rosie collected her things together and went back downstairs.

"I've seen that face before," said Alannah. "It's the same expression as Michael's on his leaving day. I'm so sorry – it must be so hard for you."

"It is," she said. "I'm looking forward to going home and seeing my family. Especially Mollie, my sister. I've missed her a lot. She would have loved it here."

"Are we ready?" asked Thumblerock as he came into the kitchen.

"As I'll ever be," said Rosie. Alannah laughed.

"What a cute expression. Perfect for this situation I suppose." They went out to the carriage where Alannah knelt and hugged Rosie. "Thank you for being such a brave and beautiful companion. It's been a real pleasure to have you amongst us, and we will all miss you terribly. The animals are distraught that you're leaving – it's hard for them, too." As Rosie began to cry, Alannah produced a cotton tissue from her pocket and dabbed her eyes. "We need you to be brave."

"I know, I'm sorry," she said. "I won't forget you. Be safe, and tell Rocky to give up this job and be by your side."

Alannah laughed. "Rocky told me about your job replacement plan with Maia. Don't worry, I'll work on him." She helped Rosie into the carriage and stood back as Thumblerock jumped in before it started to slowly roll away.

"Wait," said Rosie. "Where's Hattie?" Hattie came charging out of the kitchen and leapt into the carriage. "We nearly left you." She raised her head, grumbled and then barked. Alannah and Thumblerock laughed at what Hattie said as the carriage pulled away.

"I'll miss you as well, Hattie," said Alannah, waving.

Rosie waved until she was out of sight and then turned to face the road ahead. "So, I'll be back on Earth about half an hour after we left?"

"You will," said Thumblerock. "So don't worry; your grandma will be none the wiser."

"It's just amazing," said Rosie. "So what happens next?"

"We'll retrace our steps. We have to stop over for a few hours at the Way Station, then we'll be back on Earth tomorrow afternoon. The motivators will take care of the timings."

Rosie sat back in the carriage and watched the world pass by. A few other travellers heading in the opposite direction waved at her. With the carriage cruising along at a good pace, she could see the Damianos star starting to disappear behind the distant mountains. It would be dark soon, and they would be at that awful Way Station. She already hated that place, and she'd only been there once.

"The Way Station, Rocky, what's going on with that? I don't like it, and the banging outside. It's scary."

"I know," he said. "The cabin is still safe; nothing can get in even though they're trying."

"You won't tell me who they are will you?"

"I'd prefer not to concern you with that. The main problem is the power required to keep the station safe. It's being affected by the same issue as the Earth stream. To maintain the balance, the system is diverting power to reinforce the degradation of the stream. If you understand me?"

"I think so," she said. "So what happens in the future, to the Way Station I mean?"

"I don't know, Rosie."

They both remained quiet and thoughtful for the rest of the journey. Alannah had made some drinks and savoury snacks, which they picked at. They arrived at the portal in the dark. After Thumblerock parked the carriage, they climbed up the slope towards the old oak. Once inside, Rosie knelt with her arm around Hattie. Thumblerock linked the same way with her.

She took a tight grip around her motivator as Thumblerock said quietly, "Earth Way Station."

An explosive rainbow suddenly erupted all around them and there was an instant feeling of weightlessness as they hurtled towards their destination inside a bubble of calm.

Rosie opened her eyes to see the cabin. She stood up and led Hattie out of the fireplace. As they left, a multicoloured warming fire instantly blazed away in the hearth. Rosie sat down in a chair with Hattie by her side. She could feel tiredness washing over her and within a few minutes, they both were fast asleep.

Thumblerock studied the cabin. He was looking for evidence of other travellers passing through the station. *They must have done,* he thought to himself. *How could they have travelled to and from Earth without passing through here?* He just couldn't tell; a good job was done to hide their presence. Nothing seemed out of place.

He sat down in his chair and took out a small device from his pocket, which looked like an oval stone about the size of a matchbox. He touched it against his motivator and then let it go from the palm of his hand. It floated up with a faint whirring noise and began to focus a red strobe-like beam along all the walls and surfaces. It tracked its way around, scanning the whole area.

After a few minutes, it returned to Thumblerock's palm, and then produced a graphic three-dimensional display of the whole cabin. As careful as they'd been, three areas of the cabin showed unrecognised DNA traces from both Troll and human.

It was as he expected. The next puzzle was where they'd travelled from on Earth. He hoped it was not the portal near Rosie's grandma's home. Perhaps the infiltrators had found a way to site another portal. Although not a development the Council would like to hear, at least Rosie and her relatives would be safer if that were the case.

Thumblerock settled into his chair by the fire and threw a blanket over him. Hattie looked up and yawned with a yowl.

"Don't fret, old girl, you'll soon be home."

In that instant, a terrific bang shattered the peace inside the cabin. Rosie jumped out of her seat in terror, and Hattie was bolt upright barking. Thumblerock looked startled as well.

"It's all right," he said. "No need for panic; I expected this. They know when the cabin is occupied you see. I have a remedy of sorts that will reinforce the shell and keep them at bay."

He fished in his bag and brought out a small reel of white cord. Thumblerock started running the cord, which had an adhesive quality all around the perimeter of the cabin, until he'd completed a full circuit. He cut it and joined each end into a socket on either side of the fireplace.

Standing back, he whispered, "Activate shield."

Every part of the cord radiated a thin, colourful wave, which rose up and around the dome of the cabin until the whole area was sealed behind it.

"Don't get too close now," said Thumblerock. "It will give you a nasty shock if you touch the field."

Hattie moved further away from the fireplace and lay down by Rosie's chair. Another bang on the outside was followed by a horrific tortured scream. She had never heard anything like it. After ducking under her blanket, Thumblerock laughed out loud.

"That'll give them something to think about. It should be quiet now," he said to both of them. "You can go back to sleep." Thumblerock returned to his seat, looked carefully around the cabin's shield, grunted, and then closed his eyes.

When Rosie awoke, Thumblerock was already busy preparing some food.

"Here you are." He brought Rosie a wrap filled with a sweet crunchy salad mixed with a tangy sauce, and a glass of fruit juice.

"This is wonderful, Rocky."

"Don't thank me," he said. "Alannah prepared this for us."

They sat and ate. Hattie joined in licking her bowl clean within seconds before turning around to look at Rocky and Rosie.

"You're not having mine," said Rosie, laughing. "You'll have to wait until we get home." The dog grumbled, and then turned to her water bowl.

Twenty minutes later, they were all stood in front of the fireplace.

"What if there's someone in the tunnel when we arrive?" she asked.

"When we step into the stream, it's set to only deliver the package, which is us, if there's no activity at the destination point. If the motivator detects any movement in the vicinity, it will delay our arrival." Rosie was about to speak. "Before you ask the next question," he said, "no, we won't notice any time delay whilst we are in the stream. The motivator manipulates time, as you know, so it can adjust our arrival time. The only thing it can't do is send us back in time – that's impossible. If there's any significant delay, it just won't send us until the coast is clear. These settings can be adjusted depending on the nature of travel and the relationship with each society. The Earth is a closed world, if you understand my meaning, so travel is sensitive as far as the motivator is concerned."

"I understand, Rocky. It makes perfect sense."

"Rosie, before we go, I need to link my motivator with your Alcyone Star." Thumblerock retrieved his own little silver box and spoke to it; after which, a small green projection of symbols radiated from it. Thumblerock touched some of them with his fingers. "Can you feel that?"

"I can." Rosie giggled. "It tickles."

"Good, don't ever take it off. The next time I arrive on Earth, you will feel the same tingling. It won't matter where you are on Earth, as soon as you feel a tingling, check your timepiece. We will meet at the same time the following day in the tunnel."

"What if I can't make it? What if I'm on holiday with Mum and Dad or something?"

"Should that happen," he said, "I'll leave a message for you in the tunnel." Thumblerock took a small oval black stone from his pocket. "When we arrive in the tunnel, I'll show you a hiding place where I'll leave this communication stone. If you find it, just touch it to your star and it will play a message. If you need to leave a message, touch the stone to your star again and speak. Is that clear?"

"Yes, I understand. Do you have any idea when this might be?"

"I won't lie, Rosie, I just don't know. After leaving you, I need to investigate this conspiracy. I don't know where that will take me. Don't lose hope, though. Just remember that time passes quickly when we are travelling such huge distances. It could be weeks; it could even be years. There's also a chance it may never happen!"

Rosie, looking forlorn, hugged Thumblerock. "I'll be ready whenever you need me."

"I know." He knelt and stroked Hattie. "Goodbye, old girl."

Hattie raised her paw and put it in his hand. Rosie realised that this could well be the last time Thumblerock would ever see Hattie, and they both knew it. She was getting old. Her grey muzzle displayed that fact. He fished in his pocket and gave Hattie a chew.

"It's been a pleasure," he said. Hattie grumbled and licked the back of his hand. Thumblerock smiled. "She just told me to be careful, and can she have just one more chew? Okay, Hattie, here you go, my last one," he said, giving her a pat on the head. "Well, this is goodbye for now, Rosie. As soon as we arrive, I'll need your motivator. I'm sorry, but I have to follow the Council's instructions. I'll quickly show you the hiding place in the tunnel, then I want you to leave the tunnel immediately and go straight home. I don't want you to draw any attention to yourselves. You are just a young girl walking her dog."

"Yes, I understand." She stretched up and kissed him on the cheek. "One more thing, I was worrying about the star. Will it radiate light all the time when I'm back on Earth?"

"No, not when I've taken your motivator away. It will just imitate a piece of jewellery."

"It's been a wonderful experience," she said. "I'll cherish the memories." It was now time for Thumblerock to produce a few tears.

"Come on now," he said. "Until we meet again. Ready?"

They stepped into the fireplace and knelt. Rosie gripped her motivator with her right hand and put her left around Hattie. She heard Thumblerock whisper, "Earth."

Following a flash and what seemed like a few seconds later, they were back in the tunnel under the bridge. It was late afternoon, about half past four, just as Thumblerock had predicted.

Rosie passed her motivator to him.

"I'm just keeping it for you. "Now, look over here." Thumblerock pointed to a brick about halfway up the curved tunnel wall. "If you look carefully, the surface contains three finger holes." He pushed his large fingers in and pulled out a brick. Behind was a metal box anchored into the rock. Just then, a door swung open. "It opens because I have my motivator. You just need to touch the box with your star, and it will do the same. This is where I'll leave a communication stone if we need to." He closed the box and pushed the brick back home. "Go now, Rosie, and don't look back."

As he watched them walk away, he fished in his pocket and brought out another small oval stone, this one was a dull grey colour. He touched it to his motivator and then threw the stone onto the ground. He stepped on it, pushing it into the earth amongst the other stones.

Rosie and Hattie walked towards the light at the tunnel entrance; tears were streaming down her face. As they reached it, she heard the tinkling of bells and saw a flash of light coming from behind her. She couldn't resist a brief look. Over her shoulder, she saw Thumblerock looking at them through the flames, and then he disappeared.

They wandered back up the lonely path through the forest towards Grandma's house. They were both quiet and sombre. Grandma wasn't at home when they arrived, so they sat at the garden table.

"We need to pull ourselves together," Rosie said to Hattie.

The dog just looked straight into her eyes as she lay on the grass by her feet. She grumbled a little, got up and wandered off around the familiar trees and shrubs.

Chapter 12 Rescue Me

Just over two years had passed since Rosie had returned from Damianos. She regularly walked to the woods with Hattie and checked the box in the tunnel, even though she knew it would be empty. Her necklace was completely dormant. The end of summer was approaching, and she was due to return to school soon.

Rosie liked school; the summer holidays just went on too long for her. She was looking forward to seeing all her friends. It was a distraction – it made her almost forget about Damianos and Thumblerock, as though it had just been a dream.

Hattie was struggling to keep up with Rosie when they walked. She felt old and tired due to the arthritis in her legs, and her back ached with every step. She stubbornly insisted on accompanying Rosie whenever she walked in the woods. Rosie was aware of this; Grandma had sat them all down a week or so ago to discuss Hattie's prognosis. They knew she couldn't go on for ever; the pain would eventually become too much for her.

Rosie was sitting in Grandma's garden painting a picture of a lake with two horses and a dog frolicking in the water. In fact, she'd assembled quite a portfolio of beautiful scenes since her return from Damianos.

Grandma commented as she passed, "That's another lovely scene. It looks like another world; the colours are amazing. Is that Hattie in the picture?"

"Yes," said Rosie.

"You're so talented. You could be a professional artist if you wanted to be." Rosie laughed.

"They're just for me, Grandma. I prefer it that way."

She was sitting in bed at Grandma's that night when the necklace started to vibrate. Rosie's heart took a huge leap – Rocky must be in the tunnel. She checked her watch; it was half past ten and completely dark. She was tempted to jump up and rush to the forest. No, she stopped herself, as that's not what was agreed. He would return at the same time tomorrow night, where she and Hattie would be waiting.

Her mind started to race; sleep would be impossible. She lay there with all the memories flooding back through her mind. How long she'd waited for this to happen. Her necklace was now dormant again. He'd left, returning to that awful moon, she assumed. A frustrating wait lay in front of her; the night dragged on as she watched the clock. She didn't remember falling asleep, though she must have done as when she awoke, the morning sunlight was shining through a crack in the curtains.

After breakfast, she accompanied Grandma to the village with Hattie in tow. The vet wanted to check her over, and then they would do some shopping.

"Are you feeling all right today, Rosie?" asked Grandma. "You seem a little tired."

"I'm fine, just a lot on my mind with school coming. I can't wait to go back and see all my friends. I'm just a little nervous about it. Don't worry."

"I'm sure you'll enjoy it once you are there," said Grandma.

The afternoon waned into evening, and they took tea in the garden before watching some telly.

"Well, I don't know about you, Rosie, but I'm going to get ready for bed."

"I'll just stay down here for a while, Grandma, to keep Hattie company and there's a programme I'd like to watch."

"Okay, sweetheart. Before you come up, let Hattie out for a last wee and lock the back door, will you?"

"Of course, Grandma. Goodnight."

When all was quiet upstairs, Rosie packed her walking bag with everything she could think of. She took some food for Hattie, some snacks for herself, including some chocolate bars, and her mobile phone. She never went anywhere without that. A torch, a compass, which was in the bag anyway, some gloves and a scarf, just in case. At quarter past ten, they slipped quietly out through the back door, locked it, hid the key in its hiding place, and crept up the garden path and through the back gate, which squeaked.

"Shush," said Rosie to the gate, which completely ignored her.

Hurrying along through the wood, Rosie lit the path in front of them with her torch. Hattie was struggling to keep up, but she was determined; she knew something was afoot. Rosie's necklace started to vibrate again, sending a thrill through her body.

"Thumblerock's coming, Hattie."

The dog stared up at her whilst trotting along at her top speed. The bridge was ahead. They scrambled down the edge and parted the overhanging vines. As they entered the tunnel, there was Maia standing in front of them.

"Maia," exclaimed Rosie, and ran to hug her. "Oh, it's so good to see you. I can't believe it, but where's Rocky?"

"That's why I'm here. Something has gone wrong."

Rosie could see the worry on Maia's face. "Is he all right? What's happened?"

"Hello, you must be Hattie?" Maia knelt and rubbed Hattie's head; she was standing there waiting to be introduced. "I'd prefer not to stay and talk here. Will you come with me back to the Way Station and I'll tell you what I know?"

"Of course, Maia. We're ready. I don't have a motivator, though; Rocky took it away with him."

"I have one for you. It's not your original; it's one of the motivators Rocky found. You remember, the one that works without a genetic tag. Rocky gave it to me the last time we met."

Maia handed her the motivator, which instantly burst into life at Rosie's touch. A static charge rippled through her hand, along with a rainbow wave of beautiful colour and a distant sound of tiny bells.

As they took their usual positions, Maia said softly, "Earth Way Station."

A flash of colour and they appeared in the fireplace of the lonely cabin on the desolate moon. Rosie noticed that Thumblerock's force field was still flowing around the walls of the cabin; she was relieved.

"How long has passed on Earth since you last saw him?" asked Maia.

"Just over two years," said Rosie. "I was beginning to think I would never see any of you again."

Maia looked a little stressed. Some worry lines were appearing in the corner of her eyes. *She still looked stunning, though*, Rosie thought.

"For us, Rosie, it's only been a few weeks. I met with Rocky before you left the city, and he told me of his plans and how to contact you as a last resort. He gave me the motivator, just in case, he said. I didn't really know what was on his mind. He was to return you to Earth, then try to follow the conspirators. He's been missing ever since, so the Council asked me to try and find him. Apparently, he'd already agreed with them that I was to be his replacement after this situation was resolved. I never knew he was my mentor, Rosie, and championing my cause within the Council. Now I'm frightened for his safety. Alannah is beside herself with worry."

"You've seen Alannah?" asked Rosie.

"Yes, I went straight to see her before coming here. She's told me everything she knows. I've also been to see Tauri – his friend in the service. He told him that he was going to try and use these unusual motivators to track down the conspirators. He believes they are operating from somewhere on Earth. That's not all, though; this situation is getting out of hand. The Council can't track any travel from these motivators, and the power degradation problem still exists. They've told me that we only have three days before they're going to destroy this Way Station. It's the only way they can see to cut the Earth off from the network and solve the problem."

Rosie looked shocked; she was trying to be calm and think.

"I've come to see if you can help?" said Maia. "It's your world, and Rocky believes you're a valuable asset. You may not know it, but he's been challenging the Council every step of the way. He believes the Earth should be helped to avoid an environmental catastrophe."

"I know he's been on my side all the way, Maia. It's not because he's told me, it's just his actions and general attitude. I knew he was unhappy and frustrated with the situation. It's kind of all irrelevant now if the Council destroy the Way Station – it's academic. Let's just find Thumblerock. Do you agree, Hattie?"

Hattie barked and spun around.

"Let's talk this through," said Rosie. "If Thumblerock used this motivator, or one like it to follow the trail, then we must do the same. Can one motivator take the lead in its destination choice? What I mean is, can we instruct this motivator to take us to Earth and yours will follow it, so we all go to the same location?"

"Yes," said Maia. "If you ask it to take you to Earth and we are all linked, then my motivator will just follow the same instruction."

"I'm just thinking out loud. There could be another portal on Earth that this motivator is tuned in to. It's the only explanation. That's why Rocky gave it to you – it must be."

"It's a good plan," said Maia. "We don't know what their Earth destination is called, though. Maybe if we ask it to send us to Earth, its memory should take us to its origin point. We'll give it a try. First, some rest and I'll prepare some food."

Suddenly, a loud bang from outside and another unearthly scream startled them.

"I hate this place, Maia. If it cuts Earth off from the network it may be a blessing in disguise. I'd hate for whatever's out there to get onto Earth."

"I agree wholeheartedly. We'll leave just as soon as we can, and by my reckoning that's about four hours from now." Rosie looked at her watch, which showed two a.m. Earth time.

Rosie and Maia tried to relax and get some sleep. Hattie, restless and grumbling, followed scents around the cabin, then returned to Rosie and barked.

"She can smell Thumblerock," said Maia. "She thinks he's been here quite recently."

"Hattie," said Rosie, "don't worry, we'll find him. Go and lie down in front of the fire and be quiet now." Hattie sloped off grumbling but did what she was told.

A few hours later, they were rushing around tidying up in preparation for the trip back to Earth. They collected in the fireplace and looped arms.

Rosie took a firm hold of Hattie and said, "Earth." With the usual wild explosion of colour, they hurtled away from the dark moon.

They arrived somewhere pitch black and cold. Definitely not the tunnel near Grandma's.

"Why does it always have to be cold?" whispered Rosie. She struggled with her bag looking for a torch. Maia produced a light first.

"We'll use this," she whispered. "The light can't be detected by normal eyesight. Just in case we're not alone." Maia shone the light unit, illuminating what seemed to be the inside of a cave. "This way."

Rosie and Hattie followed close behind Maia as she picked her way along a tunnel. The walls were damp with dripping water and a cold wind was blowing right in their faces. Ahead, they could see light; they approached it cautiously.

They came out of the tunnel in a deep rocky ravine. A stream spilt out of the cave with them and dropped down into a broader gushing brook. The sun was just rising. Rosie looked at her watch to see that it was half past four in the morning.

"There doesn't seem to be anyone around," said Maia. "It doesn't surprise me; they've chosen a well-hidden portal. A secretive traveller would not want to hang around and draw attention to its purpose. This place is perfect."

Rosie asked Hattie, "Can you pick up Rocky's scent?" Her barked echoed all around the ravine.

"Quietly now," said Maia. Hattie grumbled. "Yes, Rosie, she seems to have picked up a trail. It leads off down the ravine. He's definitely been here."

Hattie took the lead and scrambled down the rocky path, but then became frustrated having to wait for them to catch up. She was excited at smelling Thumblerock's scent. Her aching legs were forgotten for the moment.

After a few minutes of scrabbling across rocks, they emerged from the ravine into a broad valley with mountains on three sides.

"This is a stunning landscape," said Maia. "It's very old. Look at those rock formations and that huge granite mountain ahead of us." Rosie stared at the vista in front of her.

"I know this place, Maia. My grandfather has shown me pictures of this on his computer. It's where they come fishing. We're in north-west Scotland, and that mountain there is called Suilven."

"It's all making sense," said Maia. "This area and its geology would be a prime location to find the motivator crystal. The rock formations are very old and have been forced up to the surface billions of years ago by the pressure from the mantle. I expect there must be a mine here somewhere. They'll be following the rock formations, which could lead them to discovering the crystal. This is what it's all about, Rosie. They're trying to expose the crystal here on Earth!"

Rosie's mind went into overdrive. "Won't that be dangerous for our society?"

"It will have huge implications for your race – exactly what that maybe, I can't imagine."

Hattie broke up the discussion by barking.

"Okay, Hattie, we're coming," said Rosie.

The dog took off again heading along a path, which led in the direction of Suilven. The scenery was biblical. Maia was staggered at the rugged beauty of it. Down in the valley a mile or so distant, the little A road curled around the topography. Rosie could see a car coming along it.

"That's the main way humans travel, Maia. We call them cars," said Rosie. She pointed down the valley. "They burn petrol, which is a fuel made from dead carbon lifeforms from millions of years ago."

"I understand the biology and the chemistry," said Maia. "I've studied the data concerning Earth. Humans are seen as very resourceful. Your species has developed in conjunction with the available natural resources. There are similar scenarios on other planets who haven't discovered the crystal. At some point its usefulness becomes its limiting factor, because of environmental concerns."

They pressed on; the rain and a strong wind joined in to make their progress difficult.

"This is a very underpopulated area!" shouted Rosie. "We're not likely to run into many people. I'd keep your hood up, though, I'm sure we will be ignored." Maia laughed.

Over the hill about four hundred metres in the distance was a small stone dwelling standing all alone in this epic wilderness.

"Hattie!" shouted Maia, trying to make herself heard over the wind and rain. "Can you go and check if that building is occupied? We'll wait here for you."

After running along the path towards the building in silence, Hattie scouted around the outside and sniffed at the door before returning to Rosie and Maia. "No one in," she grumbled to Maia.

"It's clear," said Maia to Rosie, so they set off towards it.

"Perhaps we can take some shelter," said Rosie as she pushed at an old brown wooden door, which swung open. "It's a bothy," she said while stepping in. "It's a refuge for walkers to get out of bad weather, or even somewhere to stay overnight."

Hattie jumped up on the bench seats around the edge of the room and peered out of the small stone windows.

"Can you keep a lookout on the paths, Hattie?" asked Maia.

She barked in agreement, and then ran backwards and forwards between the windows.

Rosie read the laminated card pinned to the wall. "We are in the Suileag Bothy in Assynt, which is this area. The path leads to either Suilven or the Glen Canisp Lodge. We should be safe here for a while," she said. "I don't expect there will be any walkers on the mountains at this time of the morning in this weather."

Maia peered out of the windows. "Rocky has been here," she said, "as well as other Trolls and some humans. Hattie can still smell the scents."

"Wow," said Rosie. "I wonder where they are now."

"Not far I expect," said Maia. "They wouldn't have created a portal too far away – it wouldn't make sense. We'll rest for half an hour; we need to find their camp whilst they are still sleeping. I don't want to put you at any more risk, Rosie. It could be dangerous. Just stay here and wait for our return."

"Not a chance," said Rosie. "Where you and Hattie go, I go."

"I thought you'd say that."

"Anyway, you may need me."

Delving into her bag, Maia brought out a small box. Inside were a few oval stones. "Let me show you this." She picked up a steely blue stone the size of a marble and touched to her motivator. Instantly, she disappeared or almost disappeared. Rosie could still see her outline shimmering if she looked hard.

"Cool," she said.

Maia deactivated it and gave it to her. "It will work with your Alcyone Star. Just touch it to turn it on or off."

Rosie did, and she could see the manipulation of light in front and all around her, like a cocoon. "Cloaking technology," she said.

"I've not heard that term before?" said Maia.

"How can I explain?" said Rosie. "In the past, probably two or three hundred years ago, people used to wear a cloak. It was a garment that just wrapped around you, like a simple coat. It was called a cloak."

"I understand," said Maia. "We call it a concealment stone. When using it you must not move when it's active, or you will give away your position."

"Got it," said Rosie. "Any other magical stones? Or a weapon to shoot the bad guys?"

Laughing, Maia said, "Let's hope it doesn't come to that."

They stayed in the bothy for a quick snack. Rosie gave Hattie some biscuits and Maia a chocolate bar.

"That's amazing," said Maia. "I've never tasted anything like it. You need to get me some more of those."

"You mustn't get hooked on Earth chocolate, Maia; it won't help your figure at all. It's packed with calories." They both laughed.

After packing up their things and heading off in the direction of Suilven, in less than a kilometre, they found what they were looking for. A pair of tall wooden gates, quite broken down but still solid enough to hide the entrance to a small quarry. They were locked with a chain and padlock. A sign showed "Warning No Entry – Disused Mine Workings".

Peering through the old doors, they could see a narrow blasted out ravine with steep straight cliffs on each side. The mine entrance was just visible in the early morning light about a hundred metres down the ravine. It was also sealed with steel gates stretching across the entrance. The yard itself had several Portakabins, one or two with lights on. Hattie started scraping away at the stones under the gate and grumbled excitedly.

"He must be in there somewhere, possibly one of those cabins," said Maia. "Quietly now, Hattie." She took out a small tool the size of a penknife and inserted it into the padlock. It instantly sprang open. She slid the chain carefully out of the eye to release the gate and pushed it open. Hanging onto it, she ushered them through, then closed it behind her. She hid the chain and padlock in the undergrowth by the side of the gate.

They squatted in a huddle to discuss their next steps. In a whisper, Maia asked Hattie to scout the cabins and find the one that Rocky was in, and then return very quietly. Off she went; her black coat was a good camouflage.

The sun had not yet climbed high enough to illuminate the ravine, and shadows still spilt across the ground. Hattie's soft paws didn't make a sound. She was about ten metres from the first cabin when the door was flung open.

Rosie gasped, while Hattie dropped to the ground and froze. Two men in military uniform as well as a Troll came out and walked across the yard towards another cabin. They went in and slammed the door.

Continuing her mission, Hattie investigated each cabin in turn before disappearing from view. Rosie and Maia sat for at least five minutes waiting and listening. Eventually, to their great relief, they saw Hattie reappear out of the gloom.

"You really had us worried there, Hattie. Where have you been?" asked Rosie.

Hattie grumbled a little, and Maia said, "He's not in the cabins; his scent leads to the mine entrance. She will show us the way."

They followed Hattie quietly around the back of the cabins, skirting the undergrowth for cover and dodging the cabin lights. It was another fifty or so metres to the mine gates. The mine itself showed no light or any sign of life inside. Maia looked at the gates to see that they were locked with sophisticated Troll locks. These were not going to be opened quickly.

After inspecting the gate, Rosie noticed a gap underneath that she thought she might be able to crawl under. "I think I can get through that gap, Maia. Hattie and I will try to find Rocky. You stay here and watch our backs." Maia laughed again.

"What a peculiar expression, but I understand. Be careful, Rosie, please."

Hattie crawled under first, and Rosie followed her. She had to force her way underneath, as the ground was wet, muddy and covered in sharp stones.

"Yuck," she said as her cold hands clawed at the ground trying to get some grip. Hattie tried to help by grabbing her hood in her mouth and pulling. "Stop it, Hattie," she whispered. "You're pulling the coat over my head."

Backing off, Hattie lay down with her head between her paws and grumbled. Rosie was wet, cold and had sore fingers but felt elated. She turned to Maia on the other side of the gates.

"Here, Rosie, take this light so you can't be seen. If I don't hear from you in fifteen minutes, I'll come after you. It may get noisy."

"Okay," said Rosie, grinning. "I'll look forward to it."

Maia sniggered quietly. "Stop making me laugh, this is serious business. While you're away, I'll work on this lock."

Rosie and Hattie disappeared inside the mine with Maia's light. They soon came upon a large metal door, which was not locked but very heavy. As Rosie pulled it open, there was a loud creaking sound and a clunk as it locked itself open with a catch in the wall. She winced and waited for any reaction from the yard but heard nothing, so she pressed on. Inside, a new concrete path had been laid, stretching down a long dark tunnel. It had a low roof but high enough so she didn't have to duck.

"Maia would have struggled in here," she said to Hattie.

Picking up the pace, Hattie trotted along in silence. Rosie, on the other hand, was making some noise with her footsteps.

"Slow down, Hattie," she said. Hattie grumbled and slowed.

They continued downwards for at least four hundred metres. Ahead, Rosie could see some light, so they crept towards it. The tunnel opened into an enormous cavern. A path led all around the perimeter, and lights were suspended in the ceiling shining down illuminating the whole area.

Recesses around the cavern walls were gated with metal cage doors, and behind these were all sorts of mining machinery. The centre of the cavern was fenced off and peering down through it, Rosie could see a deep dark hole. *No doubt the mine shaft*, she thought.

Hattie suddenly took off before Rosie could stop her. She ran nearly all the way around the perimeter, then stopped in front of a caged door on the far side and started barking.

Rosie ran after her. It was too late now if anyone was around; they would have surely heard them.

When she reached the cage, she could see a large body lying on the cold floor. Rosie gasped. It started to move, to slowly roll over. Suddenly, Thumblerock was staring at them, trying to make sense of something. His dirty bruised face quickly smiled.

"Hattie, Rosie, is that really you?"

"In the flesh," said Rosie excitedly. "We've come to rescue you. Maia is back up at the tunnel entrance. How do I get you out of here?"

Thumblerock sat up. His hands were tied, and his clothes were wet and bedraggled. He looked at her for a minute trying to think.

"Over there, it's a key box, that yellow metal cabinet on the wall. Can you see it?" he said.

"Yes," said Rosie. She ran over to it. It wasn't locked, and inside a line of keys hung on numbered hooks. Rosie looked back at the cage. Above was a number five. She selected the correct key and ran back. The key worked, and she swung the door open.

Both Rosie and Hattie ran in and jumped on Thumblerock.

"Hello, my little friends, it's so good to see you."

"Are you hurt, Rocky?" asked Rosie.

"A little bruised and beaten I suppose. How long have I been away? I can't tell down here."

"Maia said you've been missing for three weeks."

Thumblerock whistled. "Thanks for coming to my rescue."

"Thank Hattie; we couldn't have found you without her."

"Well done, my special old girl," said Rocky. He put both his grubby hands around Hattie's neck and tickled behind her ears. She barked and grumbled. "You've gained a few more grey hairs, old girl," he said.

"Yes," said Rosie, "the vet is worried about her. It's the arthritis in her back and legs; she's in a lot of pain. She's hiding it from us just now. Coming to find you has given her a new lease of life."

"We can't have that now, can we, Hattie?" said Thumblerock. "I'm sure I can help." Hattie barked. "Let's get out of here first. I have a few scores to settle."

Rosie glanced at her watch; they'd been away from Maia for nearly fifteen minutes. "Rocky, we need to go quickly. Maia said that if we didn't appear, she'd start blowing things up." Rocky laughed.

"Right then. I have another little job for you, Hattie, if you can manage? Can you run back up to Maia and tell her that we are on our way." Hattie barked and took off like a puppy.

Fishing in her bag, Rosie brought out a chocolate bar and a bottle of water. "Here you are, Rocky. Try these."

"Thank you kindly," he said. "The food here isn't too good." Rosie smiled. "Come on, let's go and create some havoc."

Rosie led the way. It was slow progress as Thumblerock was far too tall for the tunnel as well as being stiff and cold from his incarceration.

They came out of the tunnel into the early morning light and joined Maia and Hattie. Maia was overcome with emotion when she saw Thumblerock approaching.

"Hello, Maia. How's your first off-world trip going?"

Maia smiled with tears in her eyes and flung her arms around him.

"Come on now, I'm all right," he said. "How about we make some noise. Have you brought me some toys?"

"Yes," said Maia. She looked in her bag and brought out a number of objects for Thumblerock to look at.

"Good," he said. He put a number of items in his pocket, including a small weapon. "It looks early in the day," said Rocky, looking up at the cloudy sky. "What time is it here, Rosie?"

"Just coming up to six in the morning."

"Perfect. Let's give them a wake-up call."

"We saw two soldiers and a Troll when we arrived. They went to that cabin over there," said Rosie.

"Okay," said Rocky. "Here's what I want you to do. Maia, Rosie, can you take the shield cord – you know, Rosie, the stuff I used on the Earth Way Station."

"Yes, I remember," said Rosie.

"Good, can you both go separate ways all around the edge of the compound laying a thin trail and join at the entrance gates? You know what to do, Maia – activate the shield as soon as possible, then hide in the scrub and wait for my signal. Do you have a motivator, Rosie?" She fished in her pocket and passed it over to him. "Thanks," he said. "Go now as quick as you can."

Rosie and Maia took a separate reel each and set off quietly in different directions, creeping along the compound perimeter. Thumblerock tied their two strings together after they'd left.

"Hattie, come with me." They ran over behind the cabin where the soldiers and a Troll had entered. Thumblerock took an oval green stone out of his pocket that Maia had given to him and touched it to the motivator. A personal shield activated all around him. "Hattie, can you stand in front of the door and bark, just once please?" Hattie did as she was asked.

Just then, Thumblerock and Hattie could hear startled voices from inside the cabin. The door opened, and a soldier leaned out and looked at Hattie.

"It's just a dog – must have come from one of the farms or perhaps early morning walkers. Go on, shoo," said the soldier.

Hattie just looked at him and grumbled. The soldier stepped down from the cabin towards Hattie. At that moment, a huge arm grabbed him by the collar, lifted him up and hurled him away behind the cabin. The soldier landed heavily and senseless.

"Again please, Hattie?" asked Thumblerock.

After Hattie barked, the second soldier poked his head through the door. "What's going on?"

Thumblerock stepped out in front of him and to his surprise, punched him straight in the face. He collapsed spark out. Thumblerock turned to Hattie. "Thanks, old girl. Go and join the others now will you."

He then stepped into the cabin to find an old Troll sitting behind a desk.

"Good morning, Assistant Secretary."

The Troll jumped up with both surprise and fear on his face. Grabbing him by the collar, Thumblerock shoved him back into his seat.

"Thumblerock," he babbled. "You don't understand, listen to me."

Rocky walked around the desk and pulled out his small weapon. He turned a dial, pushed it into the Troll's neck and pulled the trigger. A small popping sound, and the Troll winced with pain, rubbing his neck.

"I don't understand at all, Assistant Secretary," said Thumblerock. "Until I do, you're tagged."

At that moment, the girls met at the gate with their respective cords. Maia attached each end to her motivator, causing a circular dome of shimmering rainbow colours to raise up all around the compound, effectively sealing it off from the outside world.

Back in the cabin, Thumblerock said to the Troll, "I'll deal with you later," and then stepped outside.

Two more soldiers half-dressed stumbled out of one of the other cabins and fired weapons at him. He walked towards them; they stared at him amazed and confused. He grabbed both soldiers and crashed them into each other, causing them to drop to the floor with a whimper.

Thumblerock then checked all the other cabins to make sure there were no more. He dragged all the semi-conscious bodies to one of the cabins and locked them inside.

Hattie was now running back across the compound barking with excitement.

"Let's see if we can rustle up some breakfast, shall we, Hattie?" He waved to the girls, and they came over to join him.

"I'll make sure I never make you angry, Rocky," said Rosie, grinning.

"I'm not angry, Rosie, just frustrated that I let them catch me in the first place."

"What happens next?" asked Maia.

"Breakfast I think," said Thumblerock, to which Hattie barked in agreement.

Chapter 13 Where Do We Go From Here

Rosie made Thumblerock sit down while she hunted around for some food. For all his male bravado, he looked worn out. She found some eggs and bread, which she decided to toast. Considering they laughed at the suggestion at the hotel in Sculptor, she even made him a cup of hot coffee with two sugars, Thumblerock loved it.

"I've never tasted anything like it before. Just the job."

"What's the plan now, Rocky?" asked Rosie. "I expect we'll be discovered soon?"

"It's of no consequence," said Rocky. "I'd say the secret's out already; they know about our existence. I just need to set the wheels in motion for a proper introduction. This world needs help, and we will now provide it. It should have been the Council's plan all along, but the reason why it wasn't is the Troll locked in that cabin over there. I think you'll recognise him, Rosie."

"Will I?" she said.

"Yes, it's the high and mighty Assistant Secretary. The Troll from the Council who dismissed your appeal for help at the Council meeting." Rosie and Maia were both stunned at this revelation.

"But why?" asked Maia.

"Personal gain I expect, and he's not working alone. Don't worry though, they'll all be rooted out now I have him. Have you finished breakfast, Rosie? I'd like to show you something."

"I'm ready," she said.

"Maia, can you hold the fort for a while? I need to show Rosie her future," he said, grinning. Maia looked at him a little confused.

"Where did you hear that term?" asked Rosie, laughing.

"A young Irish lad called Michael," and he grinned again. "Rosie and I are going back into the mine. Hattie. Would you mind watching the main gate for me? Let me know when their cavalry arrives?" He chuckled to himself again. Maia just shook her head.

"You're enjoying yourself, aren't you?" she asked.

Rosie and Thumblerock left the cabin with Hattie. The dog walked towards the gate as instructed, sat down just in front of the glowing shield and fixed her gaze up and down the trail. They entered the mine. Thumblerock had to bend double again all the way back down to where he'd been locked up.

"Now, Rosie, go over to the perimeter fence and look down into that deep hole and wait for me."

She did, and then watched him walk over to a bank of electrical switches. He threw all the switches to the "OFF" position. All went black for a split second until her eyes started to focus on the magnificent light show now emanating from the mineshaft in front of her. All the colours of the rainbow spilt and flowed out of the deep. They illuminated the cave walls in magnificent splendour.

The sight had an overwhelming effect on Rosie. She started to sob almost uncontrollably. Thumblerock joined her at the rails. He knelt beside her and put his arm around her.

"This is now your destiny, Rosie. We will do all in our power to make sure your world crosses this bridge to the future without falling."

They stayed there for a few minutes in silence, just marvelling at the glorious colourful shadows cast from the deep.

Hattie met them on their return to the surface. "Soldiers and big flying bird," she grumbled to Thumblerock.

"Ah, they've arrived. Good." Thumblerock walked across to the cabin where the Secretary was locked in. He dragged him out and approached the collection of soldiers now forming outside the force field. "Will you join us please, Rosie?" He beckoned her towards him. "Who's in charge here?" he asked.

A man, who wasn't a soldier and dressed a little scruffily, stepped forward. Rosie gasped as she recognised him.

"That would be me!" he shouted back. "My name is Goings!"

"Good morning, Goings. No need to shout; I'm not deaf," said Thumblerock. He continued, "There's been a change of plan, so I need you to listen and I'll tell you what's going to happen next."

The man took on an air of defiance and was about to say something, but Thumblerock stopped him.

"Just wait a moment," he turned to Rosie. "Who leads your world?"

"The Prime Minister is in charge of Britain, although there are many countries on this planet with different leaders," she said.

Thumblerock turned to face Goings again. "I need you to make the most important call of your life. Please ask your Prime Minister to be at these coordinates urgently. Would you give him your grandma's address, Rosie?"

She looked open-mouthed at Thumblerock.

"The time for secrets is now over, Rosie. I can't think of a better place to start negotiations." He turned back to Goings. "Tell your leader to clear his schedule. He will be accompanying me to a planet called Damianos in the star cluster of Pleadies. He will initially represent your planet in negotiations concerning the future of your world. Any previous arrangement you've negotiated with this renegade Troll—" he shook the Assistant Secretary whom he had a firm grip of "—are now to be considered null and void. He will be taken back to answer for his actions."

Goings opened and shut his mouth in confusion.

"What are you waiting for, Goings? Get going! You've a lot to organise. We'll meet your Prime Minister... Is that right, Rosie?"

"Yes," she said.

"We'll meet your Prime Minister at Rosie's grandma's house in two hours. What time will that be, Rosie?"

She looked at her watch. "About ten a.m."

"This event concerns all the humans of this planet. There will be no secrets or advantage to be gained by any individual territories." Thumblerock turned and led them back into the Portakabin. "Rosie, your mobile device, can you call your grandma and your parents and ask them to meet us at Grandma's?"

Looking a little dazed and confused at the suggestion, Rosie asked, "What shall I tell them?"

"The truth. That's the best place to start," he said.

Rosie took out her phone and went outside to make the calls. She rang Grandma first, knowing that she'd be wondering where she had got to that morning.

"Hello, Grandma."

"Rosie, where are you? Is Hattie with you?"

"Yes, Grandma, we went out early to meet someone."

"Who?"

"Maia and Thumblerock from the planet Damianos." Rosie waited for a response, but none came. "We are currently in Scotland, and will be back at your house by ten a.m." There was another silence, then Grandma spoke.

"Oh, thank goodness you're safe. I was starting to worry. Will you tell Rocky that I'm looking forward to seeing him again? It's been a long time." Rosie was silent for a moment.

"You've met him before, Grandma?" she asked.

"Yes, it was just before my father died, your grandfather. Anyway, it's a long story. I'll tell you all about it when I see you. Did you say about ten a.m.?"

"Yes, Grandma, and be prepared for a lot of activity outside your house. Something really big and important is about to happen."

"Good," she said. "It's about time too. All this skulking about and secrets. It's been driving me crazy. See you soon, darling."

"Wait, Grandma, just a moment. Can you ring Mum, Dad and Mollie and ask them to come round as well? I just don't know what to say to them."

"Leave it with me, darling. I understand your predicament."

Rosie finished the call and thought for a minute before going back into the cabin. "Rocky, you've met my grandma?" she asked.

He smiled broadly. "Yes, and a privilege it was for me. She's a very kind and intelligent lady."

"Why didn't you tell me?" asked Rosie.

"Because it wasn't really meant to happen. It was strictly forbidden and against Council procedures. I swore her to secrecy, and she has played her part admirably. If you had known about it, you would not have behaved as naturally as we needed you to. The data we collect as you walked on our world must be clean and uncorrupted without any outside influences. I explained this to your grandma, and she agreed."

"Why did you meet her?"

"When Michael was failing in health, he sent for me. Your grandmother knew that the stories of her father were true. He'd told her all about us. His dying request was to see me once more before he passed. I was honoured to see my old friend one last time. I'll tell you how they did it when we have more time," and he chuckled. "Maia, would you escort the Assistant Secretary back to Sculptor and inform the Secretary of the current situation? Tell her that I will be along shortly, hopefully with another representative from Earth to begin this planet's initiation into galactic society."

"She may not be too happy?" said Maia.

"She will understand that our hand has been forced and the secret is out. We must now take responsibility and demonstrate our goodwill towards this planet – one that desperately needs our help and guidance."

Maia nodded, shackled the Assistant Secretary to her and led him out of the cabin towards the force field. She activated her personal shield and one for the Assistant Secretary before stepping straight through the barrier.

A few soldiers attempted to challenge her in vain; they were both intimidated and astonished by her stature and appearance.

"Please clear the way," she said. "I'm returning this prisoner to our galactic authorities for further investigation. Any attempt to intervene would be pointless and could be potentially harmful for you. Your technology is not sufficiently advanced to prevent our departure."

The soldiers stood back after an order from their commanding officer. Maia was allowed to proceed towards the portal without further interference. The Assistant Secretary, with head bowed, stumbled along behind her.

"Well, Rosie, shall we go and see Grandma?"

"Yes, I'm really looking forward to seeing her and being able to tell my family all about my experience with you. Thank you for coming to help us, Rocky. On behalf of the people of Earth, we are so grateful."

Thumblerock, Rosie and Hattie left the cabin and walked towards the force field.

"Here, Rosie, take this personal shield." He passed her a small red stone. "Activate it, will you, and I'll clip this one to Hattie's collar? It will allow us to pass straight through the force field and also prevent any interference from the soldiers."

She did as she was asked by touching the little oval stone to one of the unusual motivators Rocky had given to her.

Off they went. Rosie followed Thumblerock gingerly through the glowing field. Hattie stood stubbornly just behind it but wouldn't come through.

"Come on, Hattie," said Rosie. "It doesn't hurt – just walk straight through."

She took a nervous step forward and stuck her nose in it. As nothing untoward happened, she walked straight through and barked.

"Well done, Hattie, good girl," said Rosie.

The officer in charge of the soldiers stepped forward in front of Thumblerock, barring his way. "We need to get into the compound to free my soldiers?"

"There will be no access to this compound until a delegation from my home planet arrives to secure this facility," said Thumblerock.

"How long will that take?" asked the soldier, looking a little concerned. Thumblerock looked at Rosie and grinned.

"You tell him, Rosie."

"I'd say about half an hour," she said to the soldier, and then laughed at his bemusement as they set off towards the portal. Rosie knew the way, so took the lead as Thumblerock was blindfolded when he was originally brought to the compound.

He marvelled at the scenery, the towering stone of Suilven rearing up from the valley floor. "I can see why they selected this area to search for the crystal."

"That's what Maia said," she replied.

Rosie found the gully that led between the mountains and towards the cave entrance. The small stream gushed its merry way down towards the valley floor. Twisting, turning and tumbling over the well-worn rocky surface. Around another corner and there it was, the cave entrance, well hidden from view behind a rocky outcrop and thick scrub.

After stopping to look in her bag for her phone, she activated the torch app. Rocky followed close behind. He was struggling a little; his legs and back were stiff from being locked in that cold, damp cage. They crept along inside the dark cave following the torch light until they arrived at the portal platform.

"How will these motivators send us to the tunnel near Grandma's?" asked Rosie.

"I'm assuming there are only two working portals on Earth," said Thumblerock. "All we need to do is request it to send us to Earth, and it should take us to the alternative portal. So, are we all ready?"

"Yes," said Rosie. She clasped the motivator in her pocket, knelt down and put her arm around Hattie, who barked and grumbled a little. She didn't like this part much.

"Earth," said Thumblerock.

A colourful flash and seconds later, they arrived in the old tunnel in the wood near Grandma's cottage. Rosie breathed in heavily; she recognised the damp scent of the wood and smiled.

"Nice to be home again," she said. "It's been an eventful morning; I'm exhausted."

They strolled out of the tunnel, and Thumblerock put his hood up, causing Rosie to laugh.

"I think you'll be noticed anyway, Rocky. You're almost twice the size of most men on Earth."

"Well, at least they might think I'm just an oddity and not an alien."

They continued along the path, passing a few people walking their dogs. They stared at the giant walking beside Rosie open-mouthed. Some turned around and hurried away, while a few started taking pictures on their mobiles, pointing and laughing. Rosie was a little ashamed of them all.

Eventually, they reached Grandma's gate. Rosie swung it open, and Hattie charged up the garden. Grandma was waiting at the back door as they came around the corner. Hurrying out to meet them, she hugged Rosie and stepped back to greet Thumblerock.

"Hello, Rocky, it's lovely to see you again."

"It's my pleasure to be back here with you on such a momentous occasion. You're looking well, Grandma." She laughed, and then invited them to sit down at the garden table.

"I'll bring some tea, and I've made some sandwiches if you're hungry."

"Perfect," said Thumblerock. "Then we'll tell you what's afoot."

"Are Mum, Dad and Mollie coming soon?" asked Rosie.

"Yes, darling, they'll be here in a few minutes I expect. They're a little confused and worried. You know what your mum's like for worrying."

"Have you told them about it all?" asked Rosie again.

"Not in so many words. I think it will all make a little more sense to hear about it from you and Rocky. Now, let me get that tea."

Grandma went back into the kitchen for a moment. Hattie came out casually and lay down between Thumblerock and Rosie. She stared up at them with her big dark eyes.

Just then, the doorbell sounded from inside the house. Hattie jumped up barking and ran into the house to see who was at the door. Some concerned voices came from inside, then Rosie's parents stepped out of the back door.

Thumblerock rose to his feet, and they stopped dead in their tracks with a look of amazement along with a little fear in their eyes.

Rosie stepped forward. "Mum, Dad, I'd like you to meet a good friend of mine. Thumblerock from the planet Damianos in the star cluster of Pleadies."

"Please call me Rocky." He stretched out his hand towards both of them. "Don't be frightened of me. I'm an envoy from my planet representing a galactic society. Rosie has been helping me over the last few years in total secrecy, as did your grandfather in a similar way. She is a credit to you both."

They took his hand a little nervously and shook it.

"Please sit, and I'll try to explain as much as I can," he offered.

Grandma came out with Mollie, Rosie's sister. "Rocky, may I introduce Mollie to you." Thumblerock bent down and swung her up into his arms.

"Hello, Mollie. Rosie's told me all about you. She says you're the perfect sister." Mollie giggled.

"You're very tall," she said in awe.

"Yes, I am on your world," said Rocky, "but there are many Trolls much taller than me on mine."

"Can I come to your world?" asked Mollie. Thumblerock laughed out loud, and they all followed.

"Always questions from this family. Well, let's see what we can do in time. I'd love to show you all my world." Thumblerock put Mollie down and sat awkwardly on a garden seat.

He proceeded to tell them all about Rosie and her great-grandfather's adventures on Damianos. He described the reasons why and also the current plan for Earth. They were all dumbfounded, looking backwards and forwards at Rosie, Grandma and Hattie in utter disbelief.

Hattie barked, grumbled and went to sit by Thumblerock.

"That's a good idea, Hattie," he said. "She's just asked me to tell you that this is all true and if you don't quite believe it, ask her to do something unusual."

"You really can talk to her?" asked Rosie's dad.

"Yes," said Thumblerock. "Ask her to prove it."

Rosie's dad looked around the garden. "Hattie, go and fetch that garden trowel over there, bring it here and drop it in this old bucket."

Hattie got up, trotted over to the trowel, picked it up, brought it over and dropped it into the bucket.

"Wow," he said. "That's just amazing."

Above them, two helicopters were searching for somewhere to land. The doorbell also rang, and Hattie rushed off again to see who it was.

"That might be the Prime Minister," said Rosie. Grandma jumped up a little flustered.

"He's coming here?"

"Yes, to see Rocky and return with him to his planet."

"I'd better make some more sandwiches," said Grandma, rushing to answer the door.

It was the police.

"We're just setting up a roadblock and securing the area. The Prime Minister will be here shortly. We need to come in and search the house."

"You'll do no such thing," said Grandma, getting a little agitated.

Thumblerock appeared behind her and gave the policeman a fright. "Just stay outside and escort your Prime Minister to the door when he arrives," he said.

The policeman, who now had backup, started to protest.

Rocky picked him up with one hand and said to his other colleagues, "You can all stand over here as I told you to, and no arguments." He put the unnerved policeman down unharmed. At that moment, Goings stepped forward.

"Do as he asks, Officer," said Goings. "Would you mind if I come in and see the family in advance of the Prime Minister's arrival?"

"Is that okay with you, Grandma?" said Thumblerock.

"Yes, yes," she said. "I know who he is."

"In you come, then," said Thumblerock. "The family is in the garden."

Goings made his way through the house, followed by Thumblerock. Grandma shut the door on the policemen and hurried off to the kitchen.

"Well, this is turning into a weird day," said Rosie's dad, as Mr Goings joined them in the garden.

"Not weird – momentous," said Thumblerock, following him out. He addressed Goings, "Is your Prime Minister ready and willing to take a trip with me?"

"He would like to ask a few questions of you first, but he's asked me to clear his diary for the next couple of weeks."

"Why?" asked Rosie. "He'll only be away for half an hour," and she smirked.

Goings looked a little perplexed.

"Rosie is correct," said Thumblerock. "Only a few days on our world and travelling faster than light speed. Do you have a grasp of physics and superluminal travel?" Goings looked blankly back at him. "Oh, never mind. It's a subject for another day."

Goings addressed Rosie. "You've travelled to this world, Rosie, would you consider them to be a peaceable society and genuine in their offers of assistance?"

Rosie looked at Goings suspiciously. "I can only answer from the experiences of myself and generations of my family. A few of us lucky ones have had to keep this special secret, and now it's time to share its wonder with the whole world."

At that moment, the doorbell rang once more, and Hattie rushed off barking to see who it was this time. Grandma followed her and opened the front door. The Prime Minister stood there flanked by two dark-suited bodyguards.

"Good morning. I'm here to see a Mr Tumblrook?"

"Thumblerock," said Grandma. "Hello, Prime Minister, would you follow me? We're all in the back garden, as well as your aide Mr Goings." They all attempted to enter. "Not you two," she said, looking at the bodyguards. The Prime Minister looked a little anxiously at them. "Mr Prime Minister," said Grandma, "do you honestly believe you're in any danger?" Thumblerock appeared in the hallway.

"Excuse me, Grandma, which one is the Prime Minister?"

"I am," he stuttered while staring up at the massive form of Thumblerock.

"Come in, then."

The Prime Minister passed under Thumblerock's arm as he held the door open. The two bodyguards tried to push past, but Thumblerock blocked their entry, shoving them both backwards before shutting the door.

The Prime Minister followed Hattie through the house and into the garden. He was relieved to see his colleague sat at the garden table talking with a young girl. There were a few other people whom he assumed were family.

"Is everything proving satisfactory and plausible, Goings?" asked the Prime Minister.

"As far as I can tell," replied his aide.

Thumblerock then came outside. "I've asked Grandma if she wouldn't mind providing some refreshments. She'll be out in a moment. To business, then," he said before addressing the Prime Minister directly. "My name is Thumblerock of the Planet Damianos. I'm here as a representative of this galaxy's society of technologically advanced races." Thumblerock took a step back from the table and pulled a gleaming blue stone from his pocket. He touched it to his motivator and then let it go. It hovered in the air for a second, after which a three-dimensional map of the entire galaxy was displayed.

The Prime Minister gasped at the pure simplicity of the technology. Rosie recognised the map with its spidery web of waving lightstreams stretching between planets.

"Here is Earth," he said, pointing out Orion's Spur and the Earth rotating out on its own. "This is my home planet in the Pleiades sector. All these connections to other planets signify their status as either full members of the galactic society or potential prospects. As you see, the Earth falls into the category of potential. Because of recent developments, we will have to bring Earth's application for membership forward with your approval. This of course is your planet's decision, Prime Minister. We will provide you with all the information necessary to brief the leaders and inhabitants of your world. Should you choose not to embark on this journey, we will sever any further links.

"We ask for no payment or reparation. The discovery of the motivator crystal on your planet will have huge implications for all the inhabitants. As guardians of this technology, we offer you our insight, our technical knowledge, and our social experience in dealing with this momentous discovery. This day could be remembered in history as the day your world took its first step towards joining the galactic community. Please do not fear us; we are a peaceful community engaged in trade and cultural exchange across the stars. We have monitored the progress of your species for many generations through your children." He turned to look at the young girl. "Rosie here has walked with us on our world; her courage and intelligence are a credit to your race."

She looked at the Prime Minister, and could see his brain churning with the advantages of him grasping the nettle and going with Thumblerock.

"How long will this trip take?" he asked.

"What's the time now?" Thumblerock asked Rosie.

"It's eleven thirty a.m."

"I can have you back here by one p.m. on this day. However, you will spend a few days on my home world."

The Prime Minister looked completely confused as he turned to his aide.

"Don't ask," said Goings. "It's all to do with travelling faster than light."

"I've cancelled all my meetings for two weeks," the Prime Minister spluttered.

"I expect you will have more important meetings to attend to on your return to Earth. I think it will be well worth the inconvenience," said Thumblerock. "Have you brought a travel bag?"

"I have," he replied.

"Are you ready to take this giant leap for mankind?" asked Thumblerock.

"He's full of clichés," said Rosie's dad, laughing.

"We know your history," said Thumblerock. "It's much studied on our world, as are all the other planets within our community." He took a deep breath before continuing, "Mr Prime Minister, I can say no more. We need to grasp the nettle while it's hot." Rosie and Grandma laughed out loud. "Is that not quite right?" he asked.

"It's close enough." Rosie smirked.

"I'm ready to go," the Prime Minister suddenly chirped in. "I have a few bits of business to discuss with my aide. Can you let me have twenty minutes?"

"Of course," said Thumblerock.

The Prime Minister and Goings got up and left the table heading towards the back door. Once they'd left, Thumblerock sat back down with a sigh.

"Let's hope his imagination and grasp of reality is sufficient to impress the Council?"

"I think you'll find he's an interesting character," said Rosie's dad.

"I wanted to talk to you all," said Thumblerock, "whilst we have a break from them. Rosie, your personal future is also in your hands. If all goes well, there will be openings for students from Earth to represent your species in the diplomatic service – once you've completed your formal education on Earth of course. You can apply for one of these training positions on Damianos. This is from the age of eighteen. It will mean you will have to attend this further learning off-world. Would this be something you would like to consider?"

Rosie ran to Thumblerock and hugged him. "Like Maia, I would love to do that. Mum, Dad, can I?"

"It's your choice, Rosie, it's your life. You'll just have to make sure you work towards that goal in school," said her mum.

"It sounds like a wonderful opportunity," said Grandma. "Mollie, would you like to do something like that when you're an adult?"

"I might," she said, being totally non-committal.

"Well, I guess there's time to think about that, Mollie," said her mum.

The doorbell rang again; this time Hattie just groaned and didn't move. Due to all this activity, she was tired now. Rosie's dad got up from the table and went to answer the door.

"There's another thing I want to ask you, Grandma," said Thumblerock. "Can I have your permission to take Hattie back with me? We have some treatments that will help her arthritis. I won't keep her longer than necessary."

"What do you think, Hattie?" said Grandma. Hattie sat up and barked. "I guess that's settled, then." Grandma laughed. "I'd like to think you could help with her pain, Rocky."

"Oh yes, we can sort that out, can't we, Hattie? There are also some friends at the farm who would love to see you again." Hattie barked excitedly and spun around.

Rosie's dad returned with the Prime Minister, Goings and two bodyguards. "They insisted on accompanying him to a gate in the woods?"

"Yes," said Thumblerock. "There's a portal there, which will take us to my home planet."

"It's so near. How did you keep this all secret, Rosie, and you, Mum?" Rosie's dad said to Grandma. "I'm struggling to believe all of this. What a secret to keep all these years."

"Come on, then. Is everyone coming to see us off, including your two stooges?" said Thumblerock.

The Prime Minister smiled, and the two stooges seemed a little embarrassed at their demotion.

"It's protocol I'm afraid," said Goings.

"Fine," said Thumblerock.

"I'll say goodbye here," said Grandma to Thumblerock. "I've seen it before as you know."

"Okay, Grandma. I'll take good care of Hattie."

"I know you will, Rocky. Give my love to Alannah. Perhaps someday we'll meet her. I'd love to hear more of my father's visits with you." Grandma watched the small entourage leave through the back gate.

"We'll be back soon, Grandma. Put the kettle on?" said Rosie.

"I'll be waiting," she said, feeling a little teary as she watched Hattie limping down the track.

So Thumblerock, the Prime Minister, his aide Goings, two security guards, Rosie, Mollie, their parents and Hattie walked towards the portal under the bridge.

"Rosie," said Thumblerock, "would you mind returning the motivator I gave you? We need them all for further study. On my next visit I'll return yours, I promise."

"Of course, Rocky." Rosie fished in her pocket and passed the little glowing silver box to him.

The Prime Minister and his aide talked continuously as they made their way towards the tunnel. Rosie listened in for a while, but it was just dull government business. As they arrived outside the tunnel entrance, the Prime Minister was sweating and pulling nervously at his shirt collar. Rosie approached him.

"Just remember, Mr Prime Minister, you're now representing the whole human race. We're all counting on you to help secure all our futures. You won't need to worry about the EU after this. The difference is that this is a union we all need to be part of."

The Prime Minister smiled and said, "I'll bear it in mind, Rosie, and thanks for doing such a good job for us."

A few minutes later, he stood nervously in the tunnel with Thumblerock and Hattie. The rest watched on as Thumblerock gave him some instructions. They all knelt, and Thumblerock put his arm around Hattie.

The Prime Minister turned to face Rosie and mouthed, "Will it hurt?"

It was too late for Rosie to reply, as dancing fireworks of all colours erupted around them, and then they were gone.

Printed in Great Britain
by Amazon

68410126R00123